violet
ON THE runway

melissa walker

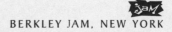

BERKLEY JAM, NEW YORK

THE BERKLEY PUBLISHING GROUP
Published by the Penguin Group
Penguin Group (USA) Inc.
375 Hudson Street, New York, New York 10014, USA
Penguin Group (Canada), 90 Eglinton Avenue East, Suite 700, Toronto, Ontario M4P 2Y3, Canada
(a division of Pearson Penguin Canada Inc.)
Penguin Books Ltd., 80 Strand, London WC2R 0RL, England
Penguin Group Ireland, 25 St. Stephen's Green, Dublin 2, Ireland (a division of Penguin Books Ltd.)
Penguin Group (Australia), 250 Camberwell Road, Camberwell, Victoria 3124, Australia
(a division of Pearson Australia Group Pty. Ltd.)
Penguin Books India Pvt. Ltd., 11 Community Centre, Panchsheel Park, New Delhi—110 017, India
Penguin Group (NZ), 67 Apollo Drive, Rosedale, North Shore 0745, Auckland, New Zealand
(a division of Pearson New Zealand Ltd.)
Penguin Books (South Africa) (Pty.) Ltd., 24 Sturdee Avenue, Rosebank, Johannesburg 2196,
South Africa

Penguin Books Ltd., Registered Offices: 80 Strand, London WC2R 0RL, England

This book is an original publication of The Berkley Publishing Group.

PRINTING HISTORY
Berkley JAM trade paperback edition / September 2007

Library of Congress Cataloging-in-Publication Data

Walker, Melissa (Melissa Carol), 1977–
    Violet on the runway / Melissa Walker. — Berkley JAM trade paperback ed.
        p. cm.
    Summary: Seventeen-year-old Violet Greenfield of Chapel Hill, North Carolina, believes herself too tall and skinny until a top modeling agent gives her the royal treatment in New York City, and Violet suddenly finds herself facing fame, popularity, and the jealousy of her best friends.
    ISBN 978-0-425-21704-7
    [1. Models (Persons)—Fiction. 2. Interpersonal relations—Fiction. 3. High schools—Fiction. 4. Schools—Fiction. 5. Self-esteem—Fiction. 6. Chapel Hill (NC)—Fiction. 7. New York (NY)—Fiction.] I. Title.

PZ7.W153625Vio 2007
[Fic]—dc22   2007014017

PRINTED IN THE UNITED STATES OF AMERICA

10 9 8 7 6 5 4 3 2

VIOLET ON THE RUNWAY

For Mom and Dad

Acknowledgments

Thanks to Kate Seaver, my editor, and Doug Stewart, my agent, for guiding me through the behind-the-scenes of the book world. Also thanks to my early readers for their encouragement, and to high school friends who always indulge my nostalgia. And to Dave.

part one

SHRINKING
violet

one

"You are beautiful and confident and wise. You handle all things with finesse and aplomb."

Okay, I'm glad Julie has a life coach who's helping her with her control issues, but the out-loud mantra thing is a little too eighties for me. Come to think of it, so is the back-to-school outfit I bought last week. Who in the world made me think I could pull off footless tights and this huge turquoise bead necklace? I'm not exactly M-K Olsen.

Getting ready for the first day of school has been angsty since kindergarten, when I let my mom talk me into wearing standard black Mary Janes instead of my sparklingly beautiful ruby slippers, thus establishing early on that I was P-L-A-I-N. Now that it's senior year, I think it's a little late to change my jeans-and-sweater image without seeming like a poseur. The thought that people might notice me for trying too hard makes me cringe, especially considering the mental list of goals I made for my last year in high school: (1) Get into college, (2) Don't grow.

I mean, emotionally I'd like to grow. You know, into a mature and graceful person, who's considerate and kind and not afraid of guys. And I'd like my hair to grow. It's been shoulder length for, like, months, and I think my follicles may be stunted. Julie says that's karma for cutting her CEO Barbie's hair down to the roots when we were six (I swear I was just going for a pixie cut I saw on Winona Ryder).

Anyway, body growth is more the kind I'd like to avoid. I pray every night that I won't get taller. Is it bad to pray only about that and not to bless my parents and my brother and my friends and starving children? Sometimes I add them in just in case someone or something is really listening. But so far, that supreme being is not paying attention to my very focused cries, because every year I look like I've gone through a taffy-pulling machine over the summer.

Last year I started as a six-foot-tall junior and I was sure that would be the end of it. But I was wrong. And so here I stand at six feet one, wearing my standard jeans (size 2, extra long) and light blue tank top (also extra long, lest my ridiculously elongated torso peek out) in the hopes that no one will notice me at all. The footless tights and chunky necklace? Made for someone cuter, smaller, and with a way more notice-me-I'm-fabulous vibe than I'll ever pull off. Someone like Julie. Or maybe Shelly Ryan.

I guess I should add that there's a number three on my mental list of goals for this year, but I'm not proud of it (and I will never tell Julie or Roger, who would skewer me with sarcastic barbs if they knew): I want to be a BK.

In a very emotional moment this summer when I was crying and obviously out of my mind, I confessed with heart-wrenching earnestness to my mom that I wanted to be a BK. She said I shouldn't have a problem getting a job at Burger King if I really went for it. That'll teach me to open up.

The three most popular girls at Chapel Hill High School call themselves the BK, which stands for the "Bee's Knees." Shelly Ryan is kind of the alpha BK; Tina Geiger and Jasmine Jostling are her drones. They walk around and twitter tooly things like, "You catch more flies with honey," flaunting their sickly sweet personas. In ninth grade, Julie and I made the comment that their fake niceness hides deadly stingers, and we thought we were totally genius for extending the metaphor. We've been making fun of them for as long as they've been ruling our school.

But the truth is, although I do think the BK girls are inane and I know high school may be their high point and I realize that in college I'll meet lots of different people who will appreciate my uniqueness and not care if I have the latest Juicy Tube color or not . . . I want to be them in the worst way. I want their glossy lips and breathy voices and fluttering eyelashes. I want their cute size 5 feet and their normal-length, bikini-ready torsos. I want their boyfriends—any of them—to know my screen name (which is just "Violet Greenfield," my real name, in case any secret admirers come looking for me). I want . . .

Ding-dong. Doorbell.

Julie. Oooh, she would be so annoyed if she could hear the internal dialogue I entertain in front of my mirror. I mean, I'm annoyed with myself. It's freaking depressing! Maybe I do need a mantra. "You are beautiful and confident and . . ." Nope, too dorky out loud.

I take one last look at the business card on the corner of my dresser that I've been struggling to ignore all morning. Yup, still there. I hesitate for a minute, then slip it inside my front pocket, just so it won't get lost.

"Bye, Dad!" I'm out the door.

I can see Julie frowning at me through the windshield of her silver VW Rabbit as I walk to the passenger side. Roger's in the backseat, as usual, playing with his PSP. At least he won't notice that I was too chicken to wear my new clothes. As I open the door, even before I drop my bag onto the floor, I interrupt the speech Julie's about to give me.

"Those tights were totally tight! And that necklace was really heavy around my neck—I mean like rocks. I'm so glad these jeans were clean."

Julie looks at me like, *Lame-o, I know you better than that*, but at least I prevent her verbal chastening. Roger does get one barb in, though.

"The tights were tight? Shock." Then, with a barely audible *tsk-tsk*, he goes back to Tokobot.

The thing is, I would have worn the outfit Julie and I picked out together, but . . . ugh. I can't even really think of a good enough reason to justify it to myself. *I'm embarrassed. I'm too tall. I don't want anyone's eyes on me, so why would I wear something colorful and trendy? That would just make people see me more.* The fact that I think this way makes me not even want to be friends with me. But there it is.

"You guys look cute," I say, hoping to divert attention from my own cowardice. Julie's wearing the silky sundress we picked out at Forever 21—ivory with golden threads embroidered throughout and an empire waist. It looks great next to her lightly tanned skin and long, dark brown hair. Not to mention her short, curvy figure.

"Julie is very Gisele at the freshman-year Oscars today," says Roger, who's in his standard uniform of Original Penguin striped tee and thrift-store corduroys.

"Don't you think you ought to start using years as references instead of the grades we were in?" I ask. "Eventually you're going to meet some people who are a different age, and they won't know what you mean."

"Hmph," Roger scoffs. "If they don't have the same pop culture calendar I do, I'm not interested."

"That's very big of you, Clark Kent," responds Julie. Roger's blue eyes have been behind black-framed glasses since he was in first grade and saw Rivers Cuomo in the "Sweater Song" video. People always make fun of him, but less so since Brooklyn-hipster style started to spread to the Carolinas. He does look like he used some extra pomade on his thick, black mop today. But at Chapel Hill High School, the jocks in weathered baseball caps still rule the hallways. In fact, my little brother, Jake, is such a basketball stud (or, as Roger likes to put it, an obsessed freak) that he actually comes in for before-school practice most days of the week. I guess it paid off, though—he made varsity this year, which is unheard of for a sophomore.

"So what are you guys's big goals for senior year?" asks Julie.

"Oh, reading a little Kerouac," starts Roger, "joining the Young Socialists Club, making sure teachers use their mixed-paper recycling bins properly, eating as many Katie's Pretzels as possible, confessing my decade-long crush to the girl I love . . ."

"No, seriously," says Julie, glaring at Roger in the rearview mirror. Sometimes she can be so bossy and controlling. "Violet?"

I pretend to ignore her, studying my face in the visor mirror as if it will somehow look prettier than it did last week. Nope—same so-pale-they're-almost-gray green eyes, pasty-and-freckled white skin, stick-out elephant ears, and tiny wire-frame glasses. Maybe I should let Roger help me pick out a cooler pair.

"Helloooo . . . Violet? Goals?" Julie's impatient with my mirror time.

"Um . . . Getting into college and avoiding the WNBA draft," I assert, not breathing a word about my treasonous BK obsession.

"You guys have no sense of ambition," says Julie, exasperated.

I give in to what she really wants. "Jules, what are your goals for senior year?"

Before I even finish my question, she's off and running: "I want to get at least a three point nine GPA, I'm retaking the SATs because, hello, I had such a horrible cold and that's why I got only a twenty-two hundred, and I'm going to make the newspaper completely unforgettable. And college. I'll get my application in to Brown really, really early. Like next week. I'm almost done with the last essay. Oh, and I'm definitely going to get a boyfriend."

Julie has this thing about wanting a boyfriend before she graduates. Although she's pretty and smart and can definitely float into that midlevel popular crowd, she's never really dated anyone seriously enough to use the word *boyfriend* (and, uh, neither have I). I think her wanting one has more to do with the iconic idea of a "high school sweetheart" than anything else. Me, I'm resigned to waiting until one of those college guys starts appreciating my uniqueness like I've heard they will.

"How about Baxter Bolton?" I ask.

Roger chortles from the backseat.

I start to whisper in my fake-sultry voice. "Oh, Baxter, the vibration is amazing when you push me against the printing press."

Roger pauses Tokobot and joins in, "Oh, Baxter, tattoo the news page across my backside, baby!"

Roger and I cackle in delight as Julie rolls her eyes and pulls into a parking space.

My stomach drops. Every weekday morning—especially this particular one, which signifies the end of summer—I hate leaving the safety of Julie and Roger in the Rabbit. I go from two understanding best friends, who find me smart and funny and outgoing, to the rest of the senior class, who—if they even know my name— refer to me as the Jolly Green Giant. Or they did, anyway, when I hit five-eight in sixth grade. That nickname has more or less worn off, but I still hear it echo in my ears as I walk down the hall trying to avoid eye contact. Julie's yank of the emergency brake is like a starting-line gun. We're here: First Day of Senior Year in High School.

two

Already speed-walking to her newspaper advisor's room for a check-in, Julie waves over her shoulder as Roger and I stroll to our lockers, both of which are in the science wing.

Last year, someone actually scrawled I ❤ VIOLET GREENFIELD in tiny letters near the top of my locker. It's not really big enough for the casual passerby to see, but that means it's not big enough for the school janitor to bother painting over, which is good. I know it sounds silly, but that little inscription means a lot to me. It's this big mystery—Who wrote it? When? Were they serious? It seemed somehow too sweetly under the radar to be a cruel joke, and I liked to imagine that Brian Radcliff penned it one day after a particularly intolerable afternoon with Shelly Ryan. Although he seems like your typical alpha-male jock, who'll drink his weight in beer next year to get into a top fraternity, I've always seen something more there. He was in my Honors English III class last year, and I swear he held my gaze one beat too long when he was presenting his original love sonnet.

"So I guess it's still there?" Roger asks.

"Huh? Oh . . ." I realize I've been tracing my finger over the laden-with-meaning ink instead of opening my locker and getting to class. "Yeah."

"Man, you are a romantic, V," he laughs. "See you on the quad fourth period?"

"Okay—have fun in physics."

As I grab my red English binder and slam my locker shut, I take one last glance. I ❤ VIOLET GREENFIELD. Sigh.

I head down the hallway—back straight, head up. At home, Mom is always saying, "Posture, princess!" and Dad loves to remark that his Violet is growing like a weed. Never funny, that joke stopped being even remotely tolerable after my big growth spurt at age eleven. When you start getting teased at school, you really don't want to hear it at home too.

Even though most people have mellowed out by senior year and I'm no longer the Jolly Green Giant, I still feel like a freak. And that may be why my natural hallway posture is bent over my books, determined not to make eye contact with anything but gray linoleum.

But today I find myself even more weirded out than usual by everyone in the hallway. Are they staring at me? Maybe my excessive self-consciousness has something to do with what happened yesterday, when I worked the afternoon shift at the movie theater.

I've worked at the Palace Theaters for almost two years now. My manager, Richard, was flitting around the lobby wearing a Burger King crown and flashing a magic wand he'd bought from the thrift shop that sits two doors down in the Palace strip mall. It had been a slow day, and my co-workers Alex and Steve—both college students—were entertaining themselves by spraying flies with gum remover (it paralyzes the poor things, but just for a few seconds). I was restocking candy.

I kind of love restocking because it is so completely mindless. Get Goobers. Line up in display window. Get Raisinettes. I had zoned out to the "I love 1983" CD that was on constant rotation in the lobby—Toto's "Africa" was on, and I was thinking of how sad it was that it wouldn't take a lot to take me away from anyone or anything in my boring little life—when I heard Joanie, the somewhat excitable overweight lady in the ticket box, arguing with a customer.

Alex and Steve, lost in the wonder of fly paralysis, paid no attention, so I peered out from behind the candy counter to see what the fuss was. A superfashionable woman in skinny jeans and a flowy top, complete with pointed boots, Chanel-logo sunglasses, and an oversized leather bag that I swear I saw in Julie's *Us Weekly* recently, was arguing with Joanie about movie times.

"Movies.com said four P.M., not three forty-five! I can show you right here on my Treo!" She was yelling so loudly that I could hear her voice from behind the glass doors. "I can't believe Mother retired to this backwards state. I want to know exactly why you people can't get online with the rest of the universe and publish correct movie times."

Joanie's shrugs and grunts of, "Well now, I just don't know . . ." were obviously not pacifying the shriek freak. I glanced over in Richard's direction—he took off his crown in a dramatic bowing gesture as he hightailed it into his office and closed the door. Typical.

Suddenly, Chanel Lady came bursting through the front entrance, still yelling at full speed. "Is there a manager here? I want to see a manager! I want to know why there aren't multiple showings at this theater—I mean, what do you do when a blockbuster comes to town? You really handle the crowds in these three rinky-dink auditoriums?"

I assumed she was addressing me, though she was flailing her arms around and not really talking to anyone in particular. Still, I felt the need to answer her, even if she meant the question to be rhetorical.

"I guess we just don't have really huge crowds," I said softly, feeling my beanpole body shrink a bit in reaction to her overt glamour. She hadn't even taken off her sunglasses inside, which seems like a movie star thing to do. Kind of asshole-y, but also pretty badass.

She didn't listen to me at all. I sometimes wonder if people like this can even hear beyond the frequency of their own shrill complaints. Chanel Lady continued to prattle on about how the Palace had the audacity to not take credit cards and how it was absolutely prehistoric not to have stadium seating. As Roger would say, *Touché*. I never watch movies here—I always go to the stadium seating theater downtown. Still, her intense diatribe was really starting to rattle me. I stared down at a row of Junior Mints as she presented grievance after grievance, wishing Steve or Alex would come to my rescue. They didn't.

When she paused for a breath, I stepped out from behind the candy counter. "Would you like to see the manager?"

I felt Chanel Lady look me up and down. It was so weird. This woman was, like, unabashedly staring at my awkwardness. I blamed the vest and bow tie—they always make me look more like a sideshow mutant than I naturally do. I mean, her gaze was excruciating.

And then Chanel Lady turned polite. "By the way," she said, as she held out her hand, "I'm Angela Blythe. And you are?" Suddenly, movie times no longer seemed important to Chanel La—I mean, Angela.

"I'm Violet Greenfield," I said, staring at her French manicure and taking her hand limply. I'm kind of hoping there's a class in college that explains how to shake someone's hand. Adults do it like it's so natural, but to me it's totally embarrassing. Angela shook really firmly. So firmly, actually, that it made me feel even more insecure about the fact that my nails were bitten down to the pink and I had ragged cuticles. "My manager's name is Richard. He's just in the office here," I said. "Um, you can follow me."

I didn't notice that this Angela woman was not following until I was about halfway across the lobby floor, which meant I had to walk clumsily back over to her. She was watching my every footstep as I returned to where she was, and when I stopped in front of her, she was still staring at me, tilting her head and even taking off her sunglasses as if to get a better look.

Julie always tells me I'm paranoid about people looking at me. I know I'm sensitive about my body. I mean, I'm so clumsy that I feel like a giraffe on roller skates. Roger called me that once, and it so perfectly described how I felt at this one junior high dance. I guess it wouldn't be so bad if I had gorgeous cheekbones or shining ingenue eyes or full lips—or some combination of those traits—to go with my bony elbows and protruding hip bones. But the whole package that is Me adds up to a disaster, and I really don't like anyone studying it.

"Umm . . . so which movie did you want to see?" I asked, trying to distract her now that her gaze was moving from my knobby knees up to my huge nose and Mickey Mouse ears.

"What? Oh, that's not important," she said, breaking her stare to rifle through her ginormous purse. "Listen, are you signed with anyone?"

"Um, signed?"

"Like an agency? I mean, I'm sure you have a local rep, but I'm talking a big agency—Ford, Elite, you know."

But I didn't know. Not a clue. And my dumb expression must have conveyed that.

"Oh, dear, you're really a gem in the rough, aren't you?"

Ew. Condescension. And by the look of the business card she was holding out, she was probably trying to sell something. People in expensive clothes are hiding something; that's what my dad says. "I'm sorry," I started, "I'm not really interested in—"

Then she steamrolled me flat.

"Oh, I should have introduced myself properly. I'm Angela Blythe, with Tryst Models. And you, Violet Greenfield, are absolutely stunning."

I looked down at the card she was waving at me.

Tryst Models, 115 Fifth Avenue, New York, NY. Before I could say anything, she was off again, talking faster than Julie does when she gets a front-page-worthy idea for the newspaper.

"Listen, are you at UNC? Wait—don't tell me you're still in high school?"

I nodded stupidly.

"Well, gorgeous, I've got fall castings coming up and I think you could be IT. And I mean IT. Are you busy next weekend? What am I saying? Of course you're not busy, you're in high school. Let me talk to your parents. I can have you on a flight Friday night and back by Sunday, just to see how they like you. But if it's up to me, Violet Greenfield, I'd say you're the next Kate Moss—but, you know, taller and without the cocaine problem . . . I hope!" Then she threw her perfectly highlighted hair back and laughed, which gave me a good look at her straight, white veneers.

So that's how I happen to have this business card in the front pocket of my jeans as I start my senior year of high school. The card of Angela Blythe from Tryst Models in New York City who wants to put me on a plane this weekend and whisk me into her world of high-heeled boots and oversized sunglasses.

And you wanna know a secret? I'm going.

(Well, after I tell my parents.)

three

Waiting out on the quad for Roger to meet
me at fourth-period lunch is painful. I'm leaning on the big tree outside the math wing as students pour out of the building, talking and
laughing and heading off to lunch in their sporty little BMWs. I'm
pretending to be concentrating really hard on a hangnail that's
clinging to the side of my thumb. Bite, look up, look down at thumb
again. Where is Roger?

"Hi, Vi." It's Shelly Ryan, with Tina and Jasmine on her designer
heels. Now, it may seem like it's cool when a popular person knows
your name and uses it, but with Shelly, there's always a backstory.

"Oh, hey, Shelly." I hide my bitten thumb behind my back and
lean farther back against the tree so I don't tower over the petite trio
in front of me.

"Gosh, is it me? Or do you look even taller and skinnier this
year?" Shelly has a way of making insults sound like compliments . . .
sort of. Tina and Jasmine stifle giggles with their manicured hands.

"I've heard any girl with your body type can model, even without an ounce of grace or poise," Shelly continues. "My mom is putting together a fashion show at University Mall, and we're looking for people to walk the runway. Tina and Jasmine are doing it—right, girls?"

"Yeah!" they both say in unison, suddenly smiling sweetly.

I am staring at them thinking, *Julie's right, it really is blank behind their eyes.* But despite the put-downs and the mannequin-like warmth and personality they're emitting, I find myself still envying the BK. And when I move to the next stage of my life, where no one knows I have dishwater-colored hair and a closet full of monochromatic sweaters, I'm going to become someone else. Someone like a BK girl—chic and confident, and maybe even a little wild. I'll wear skirts like Jasmine's, which is a blue-and-pink silk billowed style, and I'll always have my toes done like Tina's, which look deeply red and sophisticated peeking out of her peep-toe heels.

And then a sarcastic voice breaks my reverie. Thank God.

"Ladies, ladies, ladies," says Roger, bowing. "You'll have to excuse Miss Greenfield. We have a reservation at Wendy's, and they won't hold our table if we're late, I'm afraid!" He grabs my arm and pulls me away from the BK, whose smiles tighten as I leave. These girls are used to exiting conversations first, not being left. I turn around and wave at Shelly as Roger pulls, then face him and roll my eyes so he won't know that I'm secretly happy they were talking to me.

Roger and I cross the street and head downtown to Wendy's. We sit down with our bounty from the dollar menu and start unwrapping. We like to order four items—junior cheeseburger deluxe, fries, baked potato, and crispy chicken nuggets. Then we split it all and get one large Coke—the total price is around $3 each. Though my mom wouldn't be pleased, I could eat this way every day. Julie lives near campus, so sometimes we raid her fridge instead. But most days, like today, she stays at school to "do work" on the newspaper or complete applications or a project or whatever else needs to get

done. Don't ask me what she has to do on the first day of school—
that's just Julie.

"So what did the Pee's Knees want?" asks Roger.

"Oh, Mrs. Ryan is doing that mall fashion show, so Shelly was
talking to me about maybe being in it," I say. At least I think that's
what she was asking. In kind of an insulting way.

As Roger starts laughing, a piece of fry flies out of his mouth.
"Shelly really thinks she's the Heidi Klum of Chapel Hill High
School, doesn't she? Like you'd ever pimp yourself out like that."

I feel my back involuntarily stiffen. "Well, maybe I should think
about it," I say. "I mean, it could be fun."

Roger continues to chortle—he thinks I'm kidding, and he's still
amused by his Heidi Klum joke. As if he knew who she was before
Project Runway.

The thing is, I want to tell Roger about Tryst Models and Angela Blythe and how I might get to go to New York this weekend,
but I can't even really process the situation myself. Maybe the whole
thing was a joke. I mean, I did give Angela my phone number and
she hasn't called yet. Maybe Shelly set up some fancy friend of her
mother's to play a trick on me. Do adults do that kind of thing?

"I'm going back to school," I say suddenly, leaving what's left of
our fries and avoiding eye contact with Roger, who I know has his
WTF face on. "I have calculus." I walk out the door, remembering
halfway back to campus that Roger is going to be in that calculus
class with me.

Still fifteen minutes till the bell. I'm headed to my locker
when I run into Jake and his basketball friends in the hallway. Now
that my little brother is part of that crowd, neither of us is really sure
how to handle seeing each other in school. He hangs out with a lot
of seniors on the team, but those guys probably have no idea that

their beloved sophomore starter has an alien-freak sister named Violet in their class—even though I've been in school with some of them for twelve-plus years.

"Uh, hey," whispers Jake, hardly moving his lips, as the group strides past me in a wave of laughter and testosterone-charged wind. And then they're gone. None of the other guys look my way or even notice Jake giving me the barely audible acknowledgment, sans head nod.

I'm not even going to go into my internal rant about how sad it is that my little brother—who used to call me "Vi Vi" because he had trouble with Ls, who shot booger guns at passing cars with me, who buried our neighbor Joey Principetta's Pokemon cards in the yard after Joey called me an ogre—is too embarrassed to say hi around his cooler friends. Well, I guess I just did go into the rant, but whatever.

I stop by my locker and pull the Tryst card out of my pocket to make sure it's real. Yup, still there—raised navy blue lettering, stiff cream paper, cursive T logo. I hold my breath for a minute and wonder if this is the first day of the rest of my life. I'm never sure what that phrase means when I hear it in movies, but it runs through my head sometimes. Does it mean that every day is the same? Or that each dawn is a new start? Or that something is about to suddenly, drastically change?

And then Brian Radcliff walks by. "Hey, Violet."

OMG. He's talking to me. Out loud. Of course, his friends aren't around, and no one's in the hallway, so it's okay for him to say hi if no one sees us, kind of like that tree-falling-in-the-woods thing—though I can't figure out the exact meaning there either. So, did Brian really say hi to me?

"Oh, hi." I hope he said hi to me, because I just said hi in response. I cram the Tryst card back into my pocket.

"So how was your summer? Still at the Palace?"

Hello! He knows where I work. "Yeah," I say, trying to sound casual. And smart. And funny. "I'm getting to be an expert at buttering popcorn. For people I really like, I layer it." Uh-oh—rambleville. "I fill a bag halfway and then butter it, then fill it to the top and add another portion." Like he doesn't know what *layer* means. I'm such a dumbass.

"Well, I'll have to notice how you butter popcorn for me next time," Brian says. Then he smiles. Flirtatiously? I think the smile is flirtatious!

That's when the bell rings. Damn! We were so about to have a moment. I mean, I was already having a moment, but maybe he was about to feel it too.

"Talk to you later," he says. Yes!

On the way to calculus, I reach back into my pocket. Okay, so the Tryst card is real, and Brian Radcliff might like me. I mean, I know he doesn't like like me, but he could in the future, right? After I'm an international runway sensation. Wait—did I just allow myself to entertain that notion?

Suddenly, my bag vibrates. I pull out my cell phone and risk being late to calculus (not to mention an automatic detention if I'm caught talking on a cell in the hallway). But I have to answer—the number is out of town.

"Hello?"

"My vibrant Violet," says the purring voice. Angela.

"Oh, hi."

"Listen, darling, have you spoken to your parents?"

"Um, not really," I stammer. "I mean, not yet."

"I see," says Angela. She sounds annoyed for a second, but then her voice brightens again, as if she willed herself to smile on the other end of the line. "Well, dear, let's do that tonight, shall we? My cell is on twenty-four/seven, so just have your parents call me at this number with any of their little worries and I'll put their minds at ease, okay? Then we can arrange the flights and hotel. Ciao."

"Okay." I start to ask her how I should approach my parents, what words I should use, but Angela is already gone.

"Did you guys think I sounded confident in Newspaper?" Julie asks, as she drives me and Roger home. I'm secretly glad he called shotgun because I've got a lot on my mind. "I mean, I was confident, but I want to make sure I came off as knowledgeable but not a know-it-all, authoritative but not bossy," explains Julie.

All three of us are on newspaper staff together. I'm writing for the features section and Roger is a staff photographer. Guess who talked us into it? Julie thought she'd be so busy with the newspaper that we wouldn't get to hang out as much during our senior year, which of course is the seminal year of school according to various books, songs, films—and Julie. At our school, newspaper is actually a class, and today was Julie's first official editor-in-chief moment. She was great, of course, but why does she always need that to be affirmed?

"You were awesome, Lois Lane," says Roger, turning his head to smirk at me and roll his eyes subtly in Julie's direction, so I know I'm forgiven for bolting from lunch like a psycho. Roger overlooks a lot of my insane actions, like the time I called him in tears after my Secret Santa at work gave me one of those cheese-and-meat baskets from Pepperidge Farm. He knew right away that I thought someone was making fun of my weight and hinting that I didn't eat enough, but Roger managed to convince me that people just really like little jars of mustard and cured pepperoni, and they aren't creative enough to make a good mix CD (our classic annual gift for each other).

But this time, he doesn't really know what caused my crazy

mood. I so want to tell him. And Julie. But I can't. At least, not until it's more real and for-sure happening. So I sit silently, glad that Roger is the talkative type when he's not glued to his PSP, as Julie rattles on about her AP English class, which teachers she still needs recommendations from, and why she and I should start thinking now about who we want to go to the prom with. I probably won't even go, but I already know that, obviously, I want to go with Brian. In my dreams.

Soon we're turning into Heritage Hills. Yes, my neighborhood is that hokey. All the streets are named for Revolutionary War battles—Yorktown Road, Bennington Drive, King's Mountain Court. And finally we're at my little split-level on Brandywine—last one picked up, first one dropped off.

And just because she's Julie, she starts in one more time on why she thinks I should really consider wearing the tights-and-chunky-necklace combo tomorrow. "It'll be even better, Violet, because everyone else will already have worn their best outfit on day one, and you'll show up looking amazing on day two! Totally original."

Julie never gives up. And she completely believes that one day I really will put on the chunky necklace, so to speak, and that I'll be amazing in it. *I wish I had her confidence in me*, I think, as I smile at her in the rearview mirror. She smiles too, but I can see a little disappointment and frustration in her eyes.

I slam the door of the Rabbit and wave good-bye to my two best friends. They probably assume I was quiet because I'm in one of my sour moods. Which makes sense, since school just started and that tends to depress me. But this year seems like it could be different. It feels funny to have a secret from Roger and Julie. I walk into my house pondering how to tell Mom and Dad that—no matter what, no matter how—I'm going to New York this weekend.

four

There are few things more torturous than a first-day-of-school dinner with the parents. Mom and Dad have high conversational expectations on your average Monday, but I can tell by the cloth napkins and the rarely used rainbow candles already set on our table that tonight when my parents get home they'll want an hour-by-hour replay, an analysis of teachers, and some sort of goal list.

Which is why I go straight to my room after Julie drops me off. I log on to my computer in case anyone wants to IM me (only Roger does, for no reason at all, so I ignore him), I turn up my iPod (Gwen Stefani, because I'm sort of excited today and she's always psyched, but not in an obnoxious way), and I lie back on my pink flowered bedspread (to think). My ceiling has those little popcorn balls that give it texture. I've never understood why they were popular like thirty years ago, but I do like to imagine shapes within the patterns. There are also some very old glow-in-the-dark star stickers still hanging on by one edge, so sometimes they work their way into a landscape on my ceiling, with popcorn-ball animals dancing among the near-falling stars. I've had this same ceiling view to stare at my entire life, and I wonder what it'll be like when there's a new view to ponder from my bed. What if the ceiling is just matte?

I hear Dad come home, then Mom, but they don't knock on my door. Dad works at the university—he does administrative stuff for the dean of admissions, so people at school sometimes want to ask him questions about getting into UNC (or Carolina, as people here call it). I grew up on campus, but I still think about going there, and I'm applying even though Roger tells me college should be all about finding a different world to fit into. Mom does child development research, so she's mainly around three- and four-year-olds all day. Usually Mom and Dad come into my room to say hi after they get home—which is annoying even though I know they mean well—but tonight they are busy preparing the famous Greenfield cheeseburgers. Dad makes them with bits of onion and garlic cooked in, and they are Jake's and my favorite and our traditional first-day-of-school meal. Seriously—since I started kindergarten. It's kind of stupid, but my parents seem to get a kick out of it, like they do our old brass dinner bell, which is ringing now.

As I come down the stairs, Mom is exiting the kitchen with a tray of burgers. She's wearing an apron and oven mitts as if she actually did more than make the salad. Dad follows with an armful of condiments—ketchup, mustard, pickles—he's the real chef in the family.

In her ironic apron (it has roses all over it and is like a throwback Donna Reed item), Mom actually looks very Nick at Nite, especially with her short brown bob and pearl earrings. "Vi! How was your first day back?" Mom's voice has a singsong quality that indicates she'll want this to be a very long, detailed conversation about my day. I'm glad that Jake will be down in a sec to take some of the heat. During basketball season, I hardly have to speak at all at the table—

he goes on and on about tournaments and stats, and I get to play supporting role. Which isn't entirely unenjoyable. Even with my own family, I'm not that into attention.

I used to be, though. When I was in elementary school we'd take these big family trips to Virginia with my aunts, uncles, and cousins. Even though the cousins were all older than me and Jake, I'd always grab my dad's video camera and make everyone star in horror movies or lip-sync to popular songs in a karaoke-style video. Sometimes I watch one of those old tapes and I can't believe that's me, directing, writing, and acting in these homemade productions (which aren't half bad, I must say, though I'd never let Julie or Roger get hold of them). So I guess I wasn't always so shy. But that was before the sixth-grade growth spurt.

I summon a smile for Mom and am about to answer her question by going into my "first day of school" speech—Spanish seems easy, calculus will be challenging, Julie wants me to write a story about cafeteria etiquette for the paper, blah, blah, blah—when Jake comes downstairs, laughing and talking into his cell phone.

"Yeah, totally. Yeah. I know. Okay, man. Late." He slides into his usual chair just as Dad brings out the salad. Mom gives Jake a mock-stern look, but he didn't technically break the no-phones-at-the-table rule—he sat down after he hung up. Lately when I look at my brother I'm often surprised at how tall he is—six feet two, to be exact. It's so unfair that height's attractive on a guy and freakish on a girl. But fair or not, my brother has become, objectively, a cute guy. He has blue eyes and not-too-clean-cut, not-too-floppy brown hair, and he wears polos and shorts almost all year round. He hasn't had a girlfriend yet—I'd know if he did—but I'm sure he'll get one soon. Sigh. How can he be so much cooler than I am?

"This year is going to rock," he says assertively, as he reaches for the biggest cheeseburger and plops it on his plate. It's so Jake to give my parents just what they want before they even ask. "We've definitely got a shot at the state title. The seniors are sick, and even some of the returning juniors can dunk."

"What about the sophomores?" Dad says, smiling. He knows Jake is the only sophomore who made varsity this year—and he's way proud. So is Mom. "Honey, do you want some milk?" She heads into the kitchen to pour a glass of the all-American drink for our all-American athlete. The scene is enough to make me want to vurp. How did I end up the lone monster in a family that belongs on a porcelain Christmas plate?

"And, Vi, how are your classes?" asks Mom, as she sits back down at the table. "Yeah," says Jake, who has meat juice dripping down his chin and is almost done with cheeseburger number one. "Is it cool being a senior?" I can't believe this is the same kid who practically snubbed me today. But we have an unspoken pact: school is school, home is home. At least I think that's our unspoken pact.

"Um, it's good," I say, knowing that *good* won't be enough for Mom. Yup, I'm getting the eyebrow raise. I launch into my prepared spiel about math, Spanish, and newspaper. "And I think I might take some more hours at the theater because I can get a ton of homework done between shows . . ."

"You should quit that job," says Jake, reaching for burger number two. "The vest they make you wear is dork city."

"Well, I don't care as much about seeming cool as you do," I say, getting some satisfaction out of seeing Jake wince. Low blow, but I can't say I'm not hurt by our hallway interaction. Mom and Dad haven't noticed the strain that's been between me and Jake for the past year or so, which is pretty typical. They're great, but not super perceptive.

And then I think of a way to bring up the topic that's been on my mind all day.

"So Shelly Ryan's mom is doing that fashion show benefit at the mall," I say.

"Oh, is that the one she does to help out the children's hospital, Jane?" Dad asks Mom. They're friendly with Mrs. Ryan, but I think that's just out of some adult sense of politeness because the woman makes Cruella DeVil look like Strawberry Shortcake.

"Yes, I think so," says Mom. She turns to me. "So did Shelly ask you to help out backstage?"

I can feel my face getting hot. I can't help it. When I get upset, I turn beet red. And I clam up. Why did I think I could even try this Tryst thing? My own mother doesn't think I'm pretty enough to hock JCPenney dresses on a mall runway!

"That sounds fun, Vi," Dad says, sensing tension in my silence. He bumps my elbow playfully. "You can work the spotlight or help the girls do quick changes? Maybe you'll even get a free outfit out of it." He smiles, and I can see the bite of salad he just took peeking through his teeth. Ew.

Are everyone's parents this clueless?

I'm sitting in the den post–apocalyptic dinner, flipping through channels. Jake is upstairs on the phone again, and Mom and Dad are cleaning up in the kitchen. One nice thing about my parents is that they consider school and homework to be our jobs, so they don't really load chores on me or Jake—even on the first day of school when they know we won't have anything to work on. But maybe I'm missing out on learning about responsibility or something. Sometimes I wonder if I'll lack a really important trait later in life that other kids have because their parents made them do the dishes after dinner.

Mom comes into the den and plops down next to me. I can hear Dad whistling as he washes, so I know she's come in here specifically to talk to me.

"Hey, Vi." She nudges my leg, but I'm still pretty upset about the dinner-table conversation. I mean, my own parents didn't even consider the option that Shelly might have actually wanted me to model in the show. I bend my leg and move it closer to my body so Mom can't touch it. That's all the clue my clueless Mom needs to know something's really wrong—and, shock, she even knows what it is. "Is this about Shelly's fashion show?"

And then I feel the lump in my throat crack. Tears, snot, gasping for breath—the whole deal. I lean into my mother's lap and say everything: how I feel weird all the time because of my body, how everyone else has something that makes them stand out but I just blend into the wall to hide the fact that I'm built like a circus thin man on stilts, how I met Angela and she saw something in me, and how I know I'm not pretty enough, but maybe I have something special for her to have invited me to New York, and how I really, really, really, really want to go.

When I stop talking and start catching my breath, Mom looks a little bewildered. I can't blame her, I guess.

"So, let me get this straight," she says, fingering the Tryst card, which I handed to her during my meltdown. "This Angela Blythe woman has invited you to New York for the weekend to meet some fashion people and possibly walk the runway for her?"

"Well, not exactly," I say, feeling like I know more about the modeling world than I thought I did (or at least more than my mom does, which probably isn't saying much). I sit up, wipe my tears away, and start explaining. "See, I'd go up there and meet designers—or maybe their assistants, I don't know—and they'd possibly hire me to be in their runway shows during Fashion Week in New York." I find myself getting more and more energetic—can Mom see how much this means to me? "And then I'd get paid and everything. But Angela would be sort of like my agent, so she'd take a percentage of what I'd get paid for, you know, hooking me up with the designers in the first place."

Mom still looks confused for a minute, but then she stands up. "Oh, Violet, I know this sounds fun to you, but you're not ready for that kind of thing." She starts to walk out of the room. As if our conversation is completely over. As if all she heard was *New York City* and *modeling* and it scared her. As if I'm like ten years old instead of seventeen. As if she didn't listen to the part about why I need to do this.

"Mom," I say, and even I am surprised at the authoritative edge my voice has. She turns around to look at me. "I've thought about this for a long time."

"Oh, right, Violet, I forgot—since yesterday." No mystery where I got my sarcastic side.

Dad walks in now, drying his hands on a red-and-white dishtowel. He glances at me, and then Mom, and I realize he must have overheard everything. But he stays silent, which is good because I'm not done talking.

"No—that's not what I mean," I say, and I'm impressed with my calm, collected tone—especially after the hysterics that just ended thirty seconds ago. "What I mean is, for a long time I've wondered if there's anything special about me. Jake has basketball and Julie has the newspaper, you and Dad have these jobs you love, and Roger is like a supergenius in school without even trying. I'm just me. I'm okay at everything, but not great at anything. What if I turn out to be great at this?"

"Honey, you're great just being you," says Dad. You'd think that parents would remember how meaningless it is when your own father says something like, "I think you're great." Weak.

"Dad, this isn't about what you think about me, or what Mom thinks about me, or what kids at school think about me—or even what Angela Blythe from Tryst Models thinks about me," I say, realizing on the fly that I have a total parent-winning point to make here. "It's about what *I* think about me. How I feel about myself.

Since I've had that Tryst card in my hand, I've felt a little more confident, a little more like I'm someone special."

"Oh, but Vi, you don't understand," says Mom, sitting back down on the couch with me. (Yes! That means the discussion is decidedly not over.) "The modeling industry is so competitive and cutthroat—no matter how gorgeous you are, they'll break down your confidence more than anything here ever could."

"I've thought about that, Mom," I say. "I know how hard it might be. But let me just see—let me just try? Dad always says, 'You never regret the things you do, only the things you don't.' "

Dad smiles sheepishly at Mom. Game, set . . .

"Okay," says Mom. "I'll call this Angela woman tomorrow and get some more details before we decide."

Match!

I run into the kitchen to grab the cordless phone. "Actually," I yell, "Angela said you can call her twenty-four/seven, and she really wants to talk to you tonight."

Mom looks up at Dad and I can tell my tag-team approach, using both rational and emotional argument, has rendered them helpless. She reminds me that calling Angela doesn't mean the answer is yes. And then she starts to dial.

five

I'm tempted to run upstairs and listen to my mom's conversation with Angela about my possibly going to New York on the upstairs line, but I also don't want to leave the room, in case Mom starts to say something stupid and I can stop her by pantomiming wildly.

Judging by the silence on the home end, though, Angela is whizzing through details and not letting Mom get a word in edgewise.

"Yes . . . That's true . . . Well, what about . . . Well, no I . . . And if . . . Of course I'd want . . . Okay . . . Yes, that makes sense . . ."

Either Angela is a great persuasion artist or a mind reader or both. I can't tell what's going on down here, so I run up to my room and pick up the phone discreetly.

"I'll just fax it over now," Angela is saying. "What was that number?"

"Well, we'll have to . . ." Mom tries to talk, but she's thwarted again.

"Oh, of course you'll look it over and have the family lawyer study it and all that—no problem!" interrupts Angela. "As long as you do it by Wednesday. I just need a signature before we book the flight for you and Violet so the agency isn't taking the risk that Violet signs with someone else while she's up in New York, you understand."

Wait—a flight for "you and Violet"?

Mom gives Angela the fax number and they're off the phone. I run downstairs.

"So . . . ?"

"You should know, Sherlock," says Mom. "I heard you pick up the line."

"Well, it *is* my business," I reason. "What did she say?"

Mom turns to Dad, who's sort of on the outside of all this. That's pretty normal for us—Mom tends to make all the decisions, and Dad only speaks up if something really, really bothers him.

"I've agreed to look over some sort of temporary contract," says Mom, talking more to Dad than to me, which is annoying. "And if we are okay with that, we can have them book tickets to New York for me and Violet." She glances at me then, and I must be making a face because she quickly adds, "There's no way you're going to New York City alone—if you go, I go with you."

I think about objecting for half a second, but New York alone sounds scary, and I'm actually glad she wants to come. Also, she's being pretty reasonable about this whole thing, lenient even, and I don't want to slow down the wave of goodwill here.

"I also told Ms. Blythe that you and I would not be accepting their offer of a hotel room," says Mom.

"So where are we gonna stay?" I ask. And as soon as the question is out of my mouth, I know the answer.

"Oh, Aunt Rita, here they come!" says Dad, springing to life and clapping his hands together with a smile. Rita is Mom's beyond eccentric older sister who lives in Brooklyn. She's a whack job who makes pottery and sells it on her front stoop. She never got married or had kids, and Mom says she thinks all the kiln heat has gone to Rita's head. When I was really young I kind of liked Rita because she'd make me little clay animals and invent stories about them— but I haven't seen her in a few years.

"That's right," says Mom. "We'll call Rita." She looks at me expectantly, but I just shrug. I mean, whatever. I'd rather stay in a nice hotel, but like I said, if Mom's letting me go to New York City, I'm not going to split hairs.

"Well, the whole thing sounds like a fun, free trip to New York—some good mother-daughter-aunt bonding," says Dad, still smiling and looking at Mom. I know they're remembering the time when I was twelve and I saw Rita smoking a joint in her back garden. I think that made Mom worry about Rita's influence on me and Jake. Not that I even really knew what a joint was back then. But still.

"I just don't want us to get too indebted to this Tryst agency," says Mom. "I don't know if we should even accept the flight, to be honest, but Angela seems to really believe in you, Vi."

I feel my face turning red again, but this time it's in a good way.

Then the fax starts beeping.

Two days have passed and I'm sitting on the couch watching morning shows and waiting for Julie to pick me up. I haven't said anything to her or Roger about New York yet, even though it's official—as of last night, I'm going. And so is Mom. But I've tried to set boundaries (Julie's life coach would be proud), and I think Mom knows that I need her to stay in the background. Like I get to go meet the designers on my own, or with Angela. Or however it works. I'm not even sure.

I look out the window for Julie's car, but it's still ten minutes till she'd be here. I feel guilty not telling my friends what's been going on. I've even had to sort of lie in front of Roger, like yesterday when we ran into Shelly, Jasmine, and Tina again as they drove off campus for lunch.

Shelly's gold BMW slowed when they saw me and Roger, and she called me over. "Good news, Violet," she said, leaning over the edge of her new convertible. Jasmine's and Tina's faces were perfect imitations of Shelly's, which Roger must have noticed because he whispered, "Jesus. Did they just get their teeth whitened together?" a little too loudly. Shelly gave him a quick, cold stare and then turned her blinding dental work—in a sweet smile, of course—back to me. "My cousin Virginia can't make it for the fashion show, so we need another girl for November seventeenth. Wanna come try out on Saturday? We're inviting anyone who's hot. Plus, you know, superskinny girls like you."

Again with the not-really-a-compliment compliment. "Um, thanks, Shelly," I said. "But . . ."

"But Violet and I will be too busy sliding down razor-blade banisters into pools of lemon juice, which is going to be much more fun than your fashion show audition," said Roger, pulling me away.

While I was going to have to say no to Shelly because of the trip to New York, I was planning on having more tact than Roger. I turned back to the stunned BK girls. "Um, I'm going out of town this weekend," I say. "Sorry, Shelly! But maybe we can do something another time?"

Then I walked away with Roger, and I could feel six crystal-blue tinted contacts fixed on my back.

"You sounded so sincere," Roger laughed. "Out of town—

nice. I hope one of their BK spies doesn't spot you at the movies on Saturday!"

"Yeah, hopefully," I said, smiling, with my stomach in knots and feeling as fake as Shelly.

I played it off yesterday, but now that I'm waiting for my friends to pick me up on my third day of deception, I'm on edge. Julie's been busy, so I haven't had to outright lie to her like I have with Roger. I'm not exactly sure what I'm afraid of. I guess I just don't want them to get excited and then be let down. I didn't even want Julie to get her hopes up about me wearing a different-style outfit on the first day of school—so how can I let her get her hopes up about *this*?

The truth is, I'm incredibly nervous. It's like I'm at school every day and I have this secret. And it's not a secret like *I have a crush on Brian Radcliff* or even *I want to be a BK*—it's a big secret. One that could change my life. Or not. I mean, maybe I'll go to New York and the casting people will be like, "We don't get it. She's ugly." Who knows what Angela's track record is with this kind of thing? She could be totally off. But she did have those Chanel sunglasses and that designer bag, so she must sort of know what she's doing, right? Maybe I have a shot.

One second I'm chewing my nails down to the pink because I just know people will laugh at me this weekend, and the next I'm acting kind of fierce and practicing my signature runway walk (Tyra says you should have one), though that side of me only comes out when I'm alone in my room. I feel like Sybil right about now. You know, the girl with multiple personalities who Sally Field played in that old movie? I used to love Sally Field because she was so cute and perky with her little flip hair—like in *Gidget* reruns. Even if the New York people do like me, I can guarantee that *perky* isn't a word they'll use.

Jake comes downstairs with a bowl of cereal and sits next to me on the couch—he doesn't have practice today, so he's riding in with me and my friends. I haven't really talked to him about any of the modeling stuff yet, but I kind of have to because I don't want him mentioning it in the car or to anyone at school. He hasn't yet, as far as I know.

"Hey, Jake," I say, scootching over so he has more room. He looks at me and grunts as he shovels more Captain Crunch into his mouth.

"Um, so you know how Mom and I are going to New York this weekend?" I say, trying to sound casual. I have to swear him to secrecy—not in a desperate "please don't tell" way but in a, like, "keep this on the down low" way, so he doesn't read too much into it.

"Yeah," he says, not taking his eyes off the *Today* show. "For your big shot at modeling."

I wonder if his tone is mocking. It's hard to tell with all the cereal crunching around in his mouth. Actually, it's probably good if he thinks it's no big deal—that'll be one less person to let down when I get rejected.

"Yeah, right," I say. "I mean, it'll be fun to see New York, but it's not like anything's going to come of it."

"You don't know that, Vi," he says, turning to look at me. "I've seen some crazy skinny models, and you're definitely crazy skinny."

"Was that a compliment?" I ask. Really, his comment could be taken either way, but something in my brother's tone made it sound almost . . . nice.

"I guess," he says. "I mean, it's cool. You never know."

"Right," I say, turning back to Matt Lauer, who's wearing an apron and covered in flour. I stare hard at the TV as if I'm completely engrossed in the salmon cakes Matt's learning how to make at seven A.M.

Jake finishes his cereal and gets up, walking toward the kitchen.

"Hey, Jake?" I say.

"Yeah?" he turns.

"I haven't really talked to Julie or Roger about any of this, so I'm just hoping you can maybe . . ."

"Don't worry, Vi. I won't say anything in the car. And my friends and I don't really talk about you," he says, walking out the door. Reassuring, but also insulting. That's my brother.

six

There's always a weird vibe in the Rabbit when Jake rides to school with us. Julie and Roger have known Jake since he was Robin to my Batman in five-year-old adventures, but now that he's a full-fledged jock, we're not really in the same crowd. And he's younger, but definitely cooler—does that make us like high school equals?

"So, Jake, I hear you guys are going to be pretty good this year." Julie has always been good at talking to my brother—she knows a bunch of his basketball friends from interviewing them for the newspaper and stuff. I really envy the way she floats from world to world.

"Yeah, I'm pretty pumped about it," says Jake. I can feel Roger recoiling at the use of the word *pumped*, but he's polite enough, because it's my brother, not to make a snide comment. "You should come to a game, Julie," continues Jake. "I mean, if you have time."

I look over at him in the backseat, and Jake is smiling at Julie in the rearview mirror. But it's not his normal smile. I can't see Julie's face from my angle, but it seems like she's smiling too. Another not-normal smile. Hello—awkward! I am sitting behind Roger, so I can't tell if he's catching this flirtation too, but not much gets by him so I assume he is. And with this new development in my world, I almost forget to remember to feel sheepish about my secret. Almost.

"We'll see," says Julie. So coy! And then she turns to me. "So what's up for the weekend, Violet? Does Richard have you working a double at the theater again?"

"Oh, um, no," I say. Now I have to choose: lie or be honest. "Actually, my mom and I are going to take a trip to New York this week-end to visit Rita." Sometimes a happy medium is the way to go.

"Aunt Rita?" Roger turns around in his seat, and I can already see the suspicion in his eyes. "You haven't seen her for like five years! Since that time you saw her smoking a joint and your mom freaked out."

"Wait a minute," says Julie. "And you didn't say anything about going to New York! You should have gone earlier so you could have back-to-school shopped at H&M for me."

"Well, it's kind of a last-minute trip," I say. "I think my mom really wants to do some bonding or something. And you know how cheap she is, so staying with Rita saves us money, I guess."

I glance nervously at Jake, but he's playing his part, looking out the window and acting completely uninterested. Or maybe he is completely uninterested. Either way, it's working.

"Yeah, my mom's getting all weird too," says Roger, turning around and leaning back in the front seat, suspicious posture disap-pearing. "It's the whole leaving-for-college thing. Parents want more quality time all of a sudden."

"Oh, Violet, will you buy me something at H&M? Please?!" Julie says.

I can't believe this. My friends, who are usually so astute, are snowed. I came up with a plausible excuse for an impromptu trip to

NYC. The new Violet is a soon-to-be international runway star and an evil genius. Or something.

The rest of the week at school went okay. Brian Radcliff hasn't said a word to me since day one in the hall, but I've seen him and Shelly fighting, which secretly makes me happy. Is it wrong to enjoy someone else's misfortune? Even if that someone else is Shelly Ryan? In English, we learned a word for when another person's bad luck makes you happy—*schadenfreude*—which Ms. Lulliver says comes from German. Roger said that figured, but he's so fascinated by World War II documentaries that he still has a thing against Germans.

That word is probably the only thing I learned in class all week because I found it apropos of my life. All I've been able to think about is what to pack for New York, how I should act, whether my hair should be up or down when I meet people. Richard even caught me practicing my runway walk at the theater during my Thursday night shift. Of course, he thought I was doing the walk for his entertainment, so he just joined me and we pivoted our hips together down the popcorn-spotted industrial carpet while he said, "Sashay, Shantee" over and over. I actually think he may have given me a few good tips, and I was feeling pretty confident all day today.

I packed my bags with my very coolest clothes—yes, even the first-day-of-school outfit that I bailed on just this Monday. I don't have many clothes that qualify as model outfits, so I'm hoping I'll have time to hit H&M before my appointments, which Angela says are all day Sunday. I tried to ask her what I should wear, but she always seems to be in such a hurry, so I let it go. I guess since she met me at the theater in a vest-and-bow-tie ensemble, it won't matter that much as long as they like my personality. I've been watching old episodes of *America's Next Top Model* to see what kinds of questions I might get asked. It seems like confidence is the most important thing on that show, which doesn't bode well for me.

And now, waiting with Mom to get off the tiny plane that just took me from Raleigh-Durham to New York's LaGuardia airport, I'm almost shaking.

"Are you okay, honey?" Mom talked my ear off the entire flight, despite the fact that I had my iPod on. She kept saying, "I know you can hear me," and she was right, though I tried to block her out. Mostly she was talking about how it was a fun opportunity no matter what happens and I shouldn't feel any pressure, blah, blah, blah.

We walk off the plane and into the terminal, where I immediately trip over some businessman's laptop power cord in the gate area. I had this whole plan in my head that as soon as I stepped on New York ground, my entire being would change—I'd walk tall and become a gazelle instead of a giraffe. So far, not happening.

"JANE! VIOLET!" Standing at the bottom of the escalator to baggage claim is my undeniable Aunt Rita. I'm enveloped in a giant, patchouli-scented hug. You know that stereotype about New Yorkers being aloof? She shatters it.

Mom had told Rita that we could find a cab from the airport, but of course she had to come herself.

"It was no problem," she says, hoisting my giant bag full of almost-trendy clothes over her shoulder. "I just took the R train to the M60 bus."

Mom's smile is tight. "We can take a cab back to Brooklyn, Rita—my treat."

"That part I knew, Jane," laughs Rita. "I'm not crazy enough to make that awful subway-to-bus trip twice!"

In the taxi, Rita sits up front and talks to the driver about where he's from and what the political situation is like in his country. It seems like what Roger would do if he were here, and I'm suddenly struck with sadness at the fact that Roger and Julie aren't experiencing this with me. I mean, not only aren't they here, but they're not even aware of what I'm doing.

The cab passes streets of brownstones like in *The Cosby Show*, and I know we're in Rita's neighborhood. But her block isn't like Clair and Cliff Huxtable's—it's a row of houses with colored siding (aluminum?). I spot the crooked front porch of her yellow "house" right away—it looks just the same as it did five years ago.

Mom pays the driver, but I see Rita hand him an extra five-dollar bill before he pulls away.

"Here we are!" says Rita, pulling my heavy bag up the steps to her door. Weblike dream catchers hang from the eaves of her porch, and I involuntarily roll my eyes. Mom catches me and puts her finger to her mouth to silence my judgment, but I see her smiling—I know she thinks her sister's weird too.

I take my bag from Rita and head to the room that Jake and I used to share. It's down on the basement level—Rita calls it the "garden floor"—and it has a door to her pottery studio in the backyard. Well, the ten-by-ten-foot sliver of space that passes for a backyard here, anyway. I have to smile at the fact that the two twin beds with patchwork quilts and Raggedy Ann and Andy dolls are still here. This place is like the land that time forgot.

"Viiiioleet!" Rita's singsong voice is worse than my mom's.

"Coming!" I head upstairs and the three of us sit at Rita's banged-up kitchen table (she says she was into shabby chic before it was trendy). Rita heats up canned chicken noodle soup, with toast, for dinner. No one on Mom's side is much of a cook.

"So here's the schedule that Angela e-mailed to me for tomorrow," says Mom, going into ultraorganized mode. "She wants us to meet her at her office at eight A.M."

"On a Saturday?!" Rita exclaims. "That's inhuman."

"I think she wants to go over some things before your appointments, Violet," says Mom, ignoring her sister.

"Aren't the appointments on Sunday?" I ask, siding with Rita and wondering why on earth a Saturday needs to commence before noon.

"Well, I can call Angela and ask her . . ." Mom begins.

"No, no, it's fine," I say. "It'll be good to get up early because then we'll have time to shop after seeing Angela. I promised Julie I'd get her something from H&M."

"Oh, you don't want to shop there," says Rita. "With all the amazing vintage stores around, why would you want to look like everyone else?"

"Maybe we can get discount Broadway tickets in the afternoon!" says Mom, lighting up. It's like Rita's not even in the room.

"Oh, nothing good's on Broadway," says Rita. "You want to get the off-off-Broadway tickets—and those you don't have to wait in line for."

I can see the color in Mom's face rising as Rita's running commentary finally gets to her. "Sure, we'll check out every option," I say, carrying my bowl and bread plate to the sink to avoid the sisterly love. I clear the rest of the table as Mom and Rita sit silently. "I'm so tired," I say. "I think I'm going to go to bed since we have to get up so early."

"Good idea," says Mom, rising and starting up the stairs to Rita's main guest room as I head down to my Raggedy Ann doll. I look back as I go to see Rita brushing the crumbs off her more-shabby-than-chic table, humming a tune as if nothing in the world ever bothers her.

As I try to fall asleep under the patchwork quilt, I concentrate on not thinking about tomorrow and seeing Angela again. I've been worried all week that she made a mistake. That the light by the movie theater concession stand wasn't good and, upon further inspection, whatever she saw in me will be gone. But I don't want to think about that—when I let my mind go to those insecure places, it takes forever to fall asleep.

I notice that Rita has glow-in-the-dark stars on her ceiling too. And as I try to find new shapes in her ceiling, I slowly nod off.

seven

115 Fifth Avenue is a tall building with re-
volving doors and a ton of security. Mom and I have to show our
IDs, sign our names, and have the guards call up to Tryst before
we're allowed through the electronic gates to the elevator bank. Angela is on the forty-fourth floor, and my ears pop as we ride up in
the elevator. There's a TV screen showing news and weather, and I
can sort of see my reflection in it.

I planned my outfit: footless navy tights under a jean skirt and a
fitted white tee, with the beige sandals I got last May (Shelly Ryan
complimented them when I wore them on the last day of school). I
pulled my wispy hair into a bun, because I've read that buns are the
most versatile hairstyle—both sloppy and chic, says *Glamour*. When
I came up for breakfast, Mom said, "You should really get dressed,
Vi—we've got to leave in twenty minutes." So that did wonders for
my self-esteem. Still, I held fast and convinced her that wearing a
formal dress to see Angela would be overkill. Looking at myself in

the screen now, though, I wonder if I should have at least worn heels or a necklace. Oh, why did I never get contacts?!

The doors swing open, and a pinch-faced receptionist sits in front of us at an expansive glass desk. She has one of those earpieces on and is talking to someone as she types, staring into the gigantic Mac screen in front of her. I'm not sure she's even aware of us until she says, "Tryst, please hold. May I help you?" in such rapid fire that I think she might still be on the phone. But she's looking at me and Mom expectantly.

"Oh, um, we're here to see Angela Blythe," Mom stammers. She's usually much more together, but I guess Tryst Models isn't exactly the room full of four-year-olds she's used to addressing. I look around and see two willowy girls draped on pastel pink couches reading magazines in the waiting area. One has incredibly pale skin and reddish brown hair down the length of her back. She's flipping through an issue of *Elle* at a quick pace, obviously not reading the articles. The other girl has darker skin—I can't really tell if she's tan or naturally brown—and she has close-cropped, bleached-blond hair. She's not even pretending to be looking at a magazine, and I can guess from the intensity of her posture—leaning forward with legs wide, elbows on knees—that she's sizing up the redhead across from her. And then she turns to look at me. Or at least I think she does. Both of the girls are wearing sunglasses, so I can't really see their eyes. Note to self: Need big sunglasses.

"Violet and Mrs. Greenfield are here," says the receptionist into her headset thingy, as she points toward the pink couches and the scary girls, indicating that we should wait there. Miss Close Crop is still staring at me as Mom and I take a seat. But I'm not under her gaze for long. Angela immediately comes striding through the glass doors opposite us and opens her arms.

"Violet! Mrs. Greenfield!" Angela's wearing a pleated cream skirt with matching blazer. I notice that without her sunglasses, she looks a little older than she did last weekend. Maybe the girls on the couch are older too.

I go in for the hug, but Angela just grabs my palms and we sort of dance awkwardly (who opens their arms if they're not going for a hug?!). I'm mortified, but Angela is still smiling brightly. My mom shakes Angela's hand, and I wonder if she notices the superhuman grip.

"Come with me, ladies. We have lots to do!" Angela is acting like our meeting is going to take all day, but I remember that she's always in a hurry, so she probably just has a lot of appointments and only like five minutes to tell me she's changed her mind about me.

As Mom and I follow Angela's shining blond ponytail through the glass doors of her office, I find myself praying this isn't the last time I'll be in the building.

After fifteen minutes in Angela's Hubba-Bubba-pink office, making sure all the papers are signed, she hands me an itinerary for the day.

Call Sheet—Violet Greenfield
9 a.m.: Hair, Vito Escobar Salon, 112 Prince
Noon: Waxing, Shobha, 595 Madison
3 p.m.: Shopping for go-see outfit, Henri Bendel, 712 Fifth Avenue
7 p.m.: Dinner with Angela, Nobu, 105 Hudson

Okay, so clearly she's not dumping me yet—but the schedule is kind of overwhelming. I'm wondering what they might do to my hair, and what the vague *waxing* means, and how exactly to pronounce *Nobu* when Angela pipes up.

"Mrs. Greenfield, feel free to indulge in any treatment you like while Violet's getting cut and colored," she says. "Everything's on Tryst, and we spare no expense for our up-and-comers."

This is all a little too MTV reality show for me. I look at Mom for some down-to-earth help, but she's smiling at Angela and saying, "Call me Jane."

"You'll have a car, of course," Angela says, briskly (is this woman ever in calm mode?). "In fact I'm sure it's waiting for you now downstairs."

And then, just like that, we're shuffled into the elevator and plunging down forty-four floors. Our limo is waiting.

Okay, so it's not quite a limo, but it's fancy. It's one of those black Cadillac-type sedans with tinted windows and leather interior. Not a car I'd like to drive, but one I don't mind being chauffeured in, for sure. I start to relax as the driver turns on the air and asks what kind of music I like. There are two Perrier bottles in cup holders waiting for me and Mom—chilled! I peek at the schedule again and let go of the Roger half of my personality that questions every step of this journey. I decide to have fun. I ask for classic rock, and the Eagles' "Peaceful Easy Feeling" comes on, which helps.

By the grin on Mom's face, I can tell that she has no problem with today's plans. "I had no idea there'd be such a fuss, Vi," she says, looking like a little kid who gets to eat cake for dinner. "Angela must really believe in you—just like I always have!"

I'm tempted to remind her that she thought I'd be working backstage at a mall fashion show just a few days ago, but I don't want to ruin the moment. We drive through New York City and I peek out at all the people walking around, the open-air cafés, the taxis honking and swerving. I strain my neck to see up to the top of some of the buildings, but I can't—they're just too tall, and dorky as it sounds, they take my breath away.

We pull up to the Vito Escobar Salon, and the driver tells us we're in Soho, which sounds incredibly cool to me, though I'm not sure what it means. A large, muscular man in a Hawaiian shirt greets us at the door with a frantic wave. "Ah, Violeta!" he yells. "Come, come. I am Vito. Angela has told me just what she wants for you."

The nerves start up again now. While Vito seems like a very nice man, I'm kind of particular about my hair. I've been growing it out for a while, trying to make it long and wispy. I really, really don't want to leave here looking like Julie's Barbie doll did after I chopped off its locks. Then I would resemble a skinny boy, which is not a look I want to try to pull off in the halls of Chapel Hill High School.

"Hi, Vito," Mom says, still with that happy glazed look on her face. "Ah, Mama Violeta! You will see Richie, just here, and he will give you whatever you like." Richie, a short, very tan man with spiky golden hair—and bleached tips—takes my mom's face between his palms and stares intently at her hazel eyes. It's like he's trying to look into her soul to find out what haircut it truly desires. "Ah! You are a pixie inside! With evening sun highlights."

If that's giving Mom what she's asked for, I hope Vito can read my mind and know that I do not want to end up looking like Peter Pan. Or even Tinkerbell, for that matter. This situation is incredibly worrisome. Mom giggles and follows Richie to the shampooing station, waving to me on the way and giving me the thumbs-up sign. Yeah, Mom, thumbs up! Is that supposed to be reassuring?

Vito turns to me and places his hand lightly but firmly on my shoulder. He guides me into a back room where a woman in a weird white jumpsuit brings tea and cookies. We sit on a light green velvet couch and Vito takes my hands in his. I'm a novice to flirting, but even I can tell that Vito has more in common with Will than Grace, so I'm not worried he's coming on to me. "Darling Violeta, what do you see for yourself?"

"Um, well, I . . ." I feel like I'm in therapy. What kind of question is that? I stare down at the encyclopedia-sized issue of *Vogue* that sits on the sleek black coffee table at my side. It seems like Vito's asking me more than what I imagine my new hairstyle might be. Is he asking about highlights, or what I hope to get from Tryst and this whole experience? Suddenly I can't believe I'm in New York City at a famous salon, talking to the famous salon owner and getting his full attention, his intense gaze on *me*. Violet Greenfield, the Jolly Green Giant, the roller-skating giraffe, the girl who grows like a weed.

I guess Vito can tell I'm having a blank moment (and/or a panic attack, I'm not really sure), so he rescues me. He reaches behind my head to pull down my intentionally messy but not sloppy bun, and he lets my hair fall around my shoulders. His eyes widen as he musses the strands. "This is beautiful!" he says. "I know what to do."

"Oh, okay, well, I don't want anything short," I say. "I mean, I've been trying to grow my hair out for a while and I don't . . ."

"Violeta, trust!" Vito brings me over to the shampooing station. We pass Mom along the way, and she and Richie are laughing together as he snip, snips her bob away. I fear for her, but once you're a mom, you can pull off really short hair. It's weird—you have to be either a mom or a total hardcore girl to work a boy cut.

Vito washes my hair himself and brings me to a thronelike chair that's separate from the rest of the salon. I try to trance out while he's working—I just have to trust him, I guess—but I can't help eagle-eyeing his every move. Still, Angela wouldn't send me to someone who'd make me look worse—that would be bad for business, right?

After an hour of snipping, with me watching in the mirror the whole time, Vito starts to dry my hair. I'm excited about the outcome—it seems like he didn't really make it shorter. In fact, as I flip my head upright after the underpart drying, I see that my hair actually looks a little bit longer than it did when I came in. Is that possible?

"Layers and waves!" shouts Vito, and Richie runs over to see the master's work.

"It's amazing, Vito," he says, crossing his arms over his chest. "Fabulous."

I have to agree. My hair looks soft and shiny, and the waves fall just below my shoulders. I guess it's the layering part that makes it look like I have more hair than the wisps I usually work with. I still look like me, though, which I'm glad of. This is exactly the hair that I could pull off in school—a better version of what I already had, but not so much change that I'll be mocked in the hallways.

"And now, we color!" says Vito. The man doesn't talk without yelling, and now I'm shaken.

"Color?" I ask, imagining the goth girls with their jet black hair (which actually looks cool on them but is something I am so not brave enough for).

"Yes!" shouts Vito. I want to say something about how I really don't mind my dishwater hair and how with the new cut it looks pretty as is, but of course, spineless wimp that I am, I stay silent as I'm whisked to yet another chair.

Richie has already mixed some sort of concoction for me, and Vito starts to immediately paint my hair with chemical-smelling paste and wrap it in foil squares. Then I notice that Mom is sitting next to me, already foiled up and letting her new highlights sink in.

"Isn't this fun, Vi?" she says. "I've never had such treatment! Wait till your father sees what Richie's doing for me!"

My knight in shining armor she is not. I decide to speak up. "Um, is it a lot of color?" I ask, afraid to hear the answer.

"Just some lowlights, precious," says Richie, leaning down toward me and speaking gently, like I'm five. "We wouldn't turn you Tina Louise red—we want you to look young and fresh. It'll be very age appropriate."

Okay, not sure who Tina Louise is, not sure what *age appropriate* means. It sounds like some lame marketing term, though I guess it's obvious enough. Still worried, I sit in my chair and say nothing. The reason I do this, I acknowledge, is because I have never once in my life looked in the mirror and liked what I saw. Not once. So if that happens again, it won't be a big disappointment.

After what seems like four hours (but is probably forty-five minutes) of pasting, drying, poking, brushing, and moussing, all with my face turned away from the big mirror (I guess Vito, like Julie, is unimpressed with my mirror obsession), he spins me around.

There's my reflection. My wiry glasses, my pale skin, my freckles, my gray-green eyes. But my hair. My hair looks like it's been shined and waxed and nurtured and thickened. Richie was right— the color change isn't insane. I mean, it's now more of a lustrous bronze than dishwater blond—brown and gold mixed together in a way that shimmers when the light hits it. And although I know I didn't miss Vito adding in major extensions or anything, it actually seems like I have more hair. I feel myself start to tear up, and Vito looks concerned.

"Is beautiful, yes?" he says.

"It is," I whisper. And I mean it. But it's also the scariest thing I've ever done. Because the way my hair looks now, it seems like I might attract attention. I've spent my whole life trying *not* to be stared at or pointed at, and this hair is for a girl who craves the spotlight. I have a feeling this change isn't the first one that's going to make me feel both elated and terrified. But it's done, and I have to figure out how to handle it.

eight

After the big hair transformation, we (that's me, Mom, and our driver, Mario) head to a salon that Mario tells us has been in *New York* magazine a bunch of times. I'm glad Mario's chatty. He makes me less nervous by cracking jokes about New York snobbery and the whole modeling world. He even tells us about his wife, Linda, who has more than twenty pairs of shoes. "She thinks she's deprived," he says, shaking his bald head. "Already my little daughter has learned to say 'Jimmy Choo.' "

When we get to the salon, I think maybe they'll wax my legs, but they start with my upper lip. I never thought I had much hair there. The only time I ever even notice the peach fuzz is in really bright sun when I study my face in Julie's passenger-side mirror, and no one else ever looks at me that closely so I never worry about it. Still, it's nice to feel the smooth skin there now, and the process isn't awful—just like pulling off a Band-Aid really fast.

When they start on my eyebrows, I pipe up a little to say that I really don't want those thin lines like you see on old movie screens and new drag queens. Greta Garbo is gorgeous, but that's not a look I can handle.

"No, no," my lady says. "Angela has told us—natural for you, with a soft edge that is very age appropriate."

There's that term again. I have to admit that when the eyebrows are done I actually look prettier. Who knew a few plucks here and there could make such a difference?

They did a good job on brows and 'stache, but I won't let them touch my bikini line. How can I? I really hate the thought of a beautician and hot wax getting to third base before an actual boy does. In true scaredy-cat fashion, I stay silent until I am on the table, then I start crying and they let me leave. Mom says I don't have to do it if I don't want to. And besides, how will Angela ever know? Time to shop.

Apparently we don't need Mario and the car because the store we're going to—Henri Bendel—is really close to the waxing place. We walk to Fifth Avenue, and all around us people are carrying large bags—brown-and-white striped, cherry red, sky blue. The whole scene, bags and people, is so elegant that it makes me uncomfortable. We pass a man in a suit talking on his cell phone, and I swear that when I walk by his eyes linger on me. And this feels different from when the new freshmen stare at me in the hallway at school because I'm so tall. It feels almost . . . admiring.

When we walk into Bendel's (Mom is calling it that for short), someone instantly offers us perfume. In fact, there are dozens of people offering us samples of lipstick, mascara, and foundation. I'm kind of disappointed that this place is like the cheesy department stores at home.

"So do we just pick something out?" I ask Mom. All day we've been driving to these locations where people just seem to know who we are and that we don't have to pay for anything. It's like some bizarre free-for-all. Mom shrugs at me as she fends off a blush-pusher.

Then, through the chatter of the Clinique ladies, I hear my name. I spot a girl with a clipboard—she can't be much older than me—in a dark green babydoll dress and low brown boots. "Violet!" Yes, she's definitely waving at me.

"Um, hi," I say when she gets to us.

"I'm Ginny Hart, your stylist for the day," she says, smiling brightly and holding out her hand for the shake that I'm so bad at. "And you are Angela's new protégé—Violet Greenfield."

I don't like the fact that this Ginny girl is near my age. There have been all these adults fussing over me today, and now she could possibly sense that I'm nothing special—that I'm completely unpopular at school. Only people near your age can really tell that kind of thing.

"Let's get upstairs!" she says, taking my elbow and leading me up a winding staircase. Mom follows us and I decide that Ginny must be at least out of college, so maybe she won't smell my D-list status.

We pass a landing filled with tons of leather purses in all sizes and colors. *Julie would be in heaven*, I think, glancing at a price tag that's dangling. $1,295! For a clutch?!

Ginny leads us to an elevator bank, and she has to use a key to get to the floor where we're going. She explains that we're heading to a private area where special clients get extra attention.

"So is this a full-time job for you, Ginny?" Mom asks. I can tell that she's also surprised that Ginny's so young—and I'm not sure she even knows what a stylist is, so I hope she doesn't embarrass me.

"Oh, no," says Ginny, smiling. "I go to Spence, but I do this on the weekends for Tryst girls. Angela likes my eye, and around Fashion Week the girls like to have an opinion on their go-see outfits. It's really important to impress on all levels so you'll make the tents."

Mom looks bewildered and I'm not sure I understood half of

what Ginny just said, but we all keep smiling and, thankfully, the elevator dings at our floor.

"Here we are," says Ginny, extending her arm like a *Price Is Right* model. Mom and I step out of the elevator and into a softly lit room with mirrors all around and four plush chairs draped with various pieces of clothing. "I picked out a few things in your size to get us started, so let's try them on and then we can raid the store for more if there's nothing you like."

We're the only people in the room, and I hear soft strains of Patti Page singing "You Belong to Me" in the background—my dad loves old music from the fifties, and so do I. As I walk to the first chair, I see myself in the mirror and am almost surprised at how pretty my hair looks. It's like I'm looking at a dream version of me—one that I'd make up in my head while staring at my glow-in-the-dark stars after a bad day at school. And now I'm supposed to try on all these new clothes while Patti plays in the background? Sigh. This is *better* than an MTV reality show.

"First," says Ginny, "I have a little surprise for you from Angela."

She hands me a small, rectangular box wrapped in stiff chocolate-colored wrapping paper with a turquoise bow.

"Angela wanted to give you these at dinner, but I told her we'd need them to see how they worked with the clothes."

I open the box to find a silver case. Inside the case is a pair of black-frame glasses kind of like Roger's, but with softer angles.

"Try them on!" says Ginny. I look at Mom and she's nodding, which makes it seem like everyone's in on this but me.

I take off my wire-framed glasses and hand them to Mom, then slip on the new pair. They're not oval and dorky like mine. In fact, they have a quiet edge to them—and a hint of red, I see, as I turn to look at myself in the mirror. I have to admit, they look amazing. The shape makes my long, thin face seem almost heart-shaped, and the frame color somehow makes my eyes look like an intensely deep green (instead of pale seasick gray like usual). I turn around to show Mom and Ginny.

"They look great, Vi!" says Mom.

"But how did . . . ?" I start to ask, and Mom interrupts.

"Angela asked us to contact your optometrist and get your prescription to her," says Mom. "Of course we'll be paying her back for them this evening. Do they feel all right?"

They do, and I can see incredibly well. I'm about to tell Mom when Ginny jumps in. "Gorgeous!" she proclaims. "The frames are called black cherry—I knew that shade would be perfect for you from the way that Angela described your coloring. And don't worry, Mrs. Greenfield, Nicole Mouret would like Violet to have the glasses for free. It'll be good publicity for them to have Tryst's new girl wearing their frames."

I wonder if I should be disturbed that there's been so much talk behind my back—descriptions of me, free glasses, transferral of medical records for God's sake? But I'm also kind of engrossed by my reflection. With my new hair and these specs, I can almost feel my confidence meter uptick an inch. But I probably won't wear these glasses to school because they're more like for special occasions, I decide. But no need to tell Ginny that, especially since she looks so pleased with herself.

"On to the clothes!" she says, and here, I can tell, is where her true passion lies.

We go through a few outfits, and all of them look kind of out there to me (tweed knickers? velvet blouses? eyelet dresses with streaming ribbons?). Now Ginny is walking around me in a circle, examining "our favorite so far" (more like *her* favorite so far) from all angles. I'm wearing a really soft blue cashmere sweater that is loose but somehow fits my body well enough to show how skinny I am, while giving me the illusion of curves. The sweater sits just below my hips, over some very tight jeans that sort of taper at the ends.

"Are these tapered jeans?" I ask hesitantly. I don't want to offend Ginny when I obviously have no style sense, but I also don't want to look clownish.

She laughs. "No, they're not tapered—they're skinny jeans, like stovepipe pants from the sixties. Very now."

Hmph. I stare at myself in the full-length triptych mirror. The jeans do go in at the bottom, which I believe is the definition of *tapered*, but apparently I'm wrong. The girl speaks a different language and I nod and smile like a foreigner. I am in her Bendel country, after all.

She must see that I look uncomfortable, though, because although I've been wearing black "Lanvin Ballets" with this outfit (Mom calls them "the cute flats"), Ginny has another idea. "Violet, if you're unsure about the jeans, let's try these." She pulls out the most amazing pair of boots I've ever seen in real life. Black-and-brown leather, knee high, with a platform heel. As I ease them over my jeans, I glance at the label—Prada. I can't believe it but chills go through my body when I see those five letters. Does that mean I'm completely shallow? Probably. But when I put them on I feel powerful, like people might respect me if I wear these. Popular people. I make a mental note to call them my "shitkickers" around Roger and never let him see the label—he'd die if he heard that I got goosebumps from designer wear.

I walk around the carpeted room and feel myself involuntarily posing in various mirrors. Normally I'd only do that kind of thing alone in my room, but I can't stop myself—it's like these boots are my magic feather.

"Yup, that's the outfit," says Ginny, smiling and clapping her hands together. It reminds me of when Julie and I were at the mall trying on first-day-of-school outfits. Was that just like a week ago? Is it possible that I'm now in a private shopping room at Henri Bendel in New York City with a stylist and a cashmere sweater and

Prada boots? I just hope I'll have the confidence to wear this outfit for my appointments tomorrow. It might be easier because no one knows me here—not like at school where everyone would realize I was trying to be someone I'm not. Here, I could be that girl . . . right?

I look over at my home-base touchstone, hoping she'll approve. Mom is staring down into her lap and I realize she's tearing up a little bit. "Oh, Vi," she says. "You're stunning."

I believe I can do this modeling thing.

At the restaurant with Angela, I'm wearing an eyelet lace babydoll dress with a black velvet ribbon tied at its empire waist and those aforementioned ballet flats. "Well, you need an outfit for Nobu," Ginny'd insisted, thrilling Mom by telling us that Robert De Niro is part owner of the restaurant. Ginny had the sweater and jeans and wonder boots messengered to Rita's house in Brooklyn so we wouldn't have to carry them. That means someone comes in a car and drives the clothes to our house for us, apparently. And Ginny talks about it like that's a normal thing, even though we have a car and Mario would be happy to watch our bags for us while we're at dinner, since he'll be waiting in the car anyway (which also makes me feel awkward). "Oh, you don't want to have to remember the bags when you're done for the night," said Ginny. "Trust me—it's cumbersome."

I feel a little weird in my dinner outfit, but I'm sort of pretending it's Halloween and I'm dressed up like a movie star, so I'd better act the part. The hostess is really nice to us and takes us right to the table where Angela is waiting. She has already ordered some specials, which is just as well, because I can't tell what anything is on the menu. But looking at the plates holding bits of fish and seaweed (I've never been a sushi fan)—even Aunt Rita's soup-and-toast dinner is looking appealing right now.

"She's dazzling, isn't she?" Angela is talking to my mother, who's thrilled with the sushi. In fact, Mom's been so starstruck all day that I wonder if I can take advantage of this rare good mood and see if I can go it alone tomorrow on the castings

"She is!" says Mom. "And, oh, the adventures we had today were just wonderful, Angela. Thank you for setting everything up."

"It's no problem at all, Jane," says Angela with a wink. "And you are drop-dead with that pixie cut!"

Mom smiles and touches the back of her hair. I realize that I've been gazing in the mirror so much today I hardly had a chance to check out Mom's new style. It really does look cute, now that I take a good look.

"I just wonder . . ." starts Mom, slowly. "I wonder what all this means for Violet. Tryst must need some of this paid back at some point. You can't possibly give this kind of treatment to every girl who you represent?"

"Not every girl," says Angela, grinning at me. "Just *the* girls. I do understand your concern, Jane, but Violet is very special. Of course, today was just groundwork for tomorrow's castings. We have to invest in her so that she'll bring us a good return by booking some runway shows."

"Violet does have school to think about," says Mom. It's like I'm not even here, but somehow I feel like we're in the middle of an adult negotiation that I don't want to take part in, so I focus on my chopsticks and stay quiet.

"Of course, of course! Fashion Week is just that—a week," says Angela, still smiling. "She'll have to miss a few days but she can write a fabulous social studies essay or something for extra credit, right, doll?"

Now her manicured nails are sweeping my hair back a bit, which feels both affectionate and aggressive. I want to tell her that social studies is more of a junior high subject, but I'm pretty sure she doesn't care about the details.

"In any case," Angela continues, "let's not get ahead of ourselves. We'll see how tomorrow goes."

"So what is tomorrow going to be like?" I ask.

"You'll meet the bookers—people who choose models to walk the runway—and the designers will be there too," explains Angela. "They'll have you try on clothes and walk for them, and they may ask you a few questions. You don't have a book—which is a portfolio of your photographs—but I've made some calls and explained that you're one of my special cases, so don't worry about that."

Suddenly my palms feel sweaty. I haven't practiced a walk or any interview questions—don't I need some sort of coach like pageant girls have? I'm so going to blow this, no matter how good my hair looks.

Angela must read the nerves in my face because she says, "Honey, don't worry. If I wanted you prepped, you'd be prepped. I want you to be you. The way you walked that day in the movie theater blew me away. And your shy, insecure personality is very *en vogue* right now with the big houses. Just be yourself."

Shy? Insecure? I don't know how many more not-really-a-compliment compliments I can take.

"I can come if you want me to, honey," Mom says. "But I'm okay with you going on your own. We were treated royally today, and Angela has promised you'll have the car tomorrow. With Mario driving, you'll be fine."

This is the same woman who fights me if I want to stay out with Julie and Roger after eleven P.M.? I'm not sure I like New York Mom. I know I said I don't want her to hover over me—I'm seventeen, I can handle this. But another part of me is pretty scared and wouldn't mind if she bullied her way into the go-sees.

"Okay, great," I say, summoning a smile and resolving to be confident tomorrow. Or . . . not be confident, if that's what Angela wants me to do.

"Don't fret, Vivacious Violet," says Angela. She really loves playing with that V. "The bookings people aren't too scary."

For the rest of dinner, Angela and my mom talk about Mom's work with children and what Chapel Hill is like. Angela acts riveted, but her laughter rings a little hollow and she keeps checking her Treo. I suddenly wish Roger were here to read the situation for me. I'm silent but no one seems to notice. When we leave, Mario is still there with the car, waiting to take us to Brooklyn. I cheer up a bit at the thought that he'll be driving me around tomorrow—I like talking to him.

"Oh, wait—I need to run back in and pee," I say, realizing that all the green tea I drank while I avoided eating raw fish must have gone right through me. I head to the restroom and wave to Angela, who's talking to the hostess. She doesn't see me, though, and when I walk past her, I hear her say, "Today, pampered like a princess, tomorrow, skewered like a little lamb."

It's entirely possible that she's talking about someone else, but when a person uses the word *skewered* and it could remotely be referring to you, you don't feel good about it. I ride home with a knot in my stomach as Mom chats with Mario. And I feel incredibly alone.

nine

Mario picks me up at ten A.M. and we drive into Manhattan. He has the full schedule of where we're going and when the appointments are, so at least I don't have to worry about that part. Angela is standing outside the first casting location on a busy street in Soho (I'm proud that I recognize this neighborhood, but it's only because Vito's salon is on this street too). She's wearing a trench coat that is so pretty it looks like a dress—it's khaki with eyelet details, cinched at the waist with a leather belt. She's furiously texting on her Treo, but she stops immediately when she sees me.

"Violet, you vixen," Angela says, as I step out of the car. Yesterday in the dressing room at Bendel's, I felt so amazing in these new glasses and leather boots, but today I feel more like a little girl playing dress-up. And since Vito wasn't around blowing my hair in a million different directions, it's looking a little limp this morning.

"Hi, Angela," I say, tugging at my sweater and trying not to trip over the curb.

She grabs a hair band out of her gigantic purse and spins me around. "Sloppy buns, darling, are *it*." Angela spends ten minutes pulling strands of my hair out of the bun "to give it a natural look," and regales me with what I guess is meant as a pep talk.

"Don't look at the other girls in there, Violet—you are so far ahead of them it's mad. Your freshness and naïveté are going to win over the designers more than their moody pouts ever will. So you just be *you*. And walk naturally, like you're on the street. Don't think—that is every model's downfall. Okay, ready? Let's go."

"Should I know who we're meeting?" I ask, lingering on the sidewalk.

"Didn't Mario give you the list? This is the Tracetown casting, and you'll be meeting Matt and Mickey, the line's designers. I'm sure there'll be some fawning assistants around too, but pay them no mind."

"But should I know something about their clothes or what the style is or what kind of models they like?"

"Darling, everybody likes fresh meat," she says. "And that's you all over." Then she smirks, winks, and opens the door.

We walk into the building, which looks like a dingy hole to me. I guess I thought it would be more like the Tryst office—elevators with TVs, pink couches, and scary skinny girls. Well, the scary skinny girls are here at least. They're lined up along the hallway, all holding leather-bound books and wearing bored expressions. Their eyes follow me and Angela as we walk past them, stepping over some of the models who are sitting on the ground. A few say hi to Angela, and she stops to give them air kisses. There are lots of types here— blondes, brunettes, redheads, girls of all races and each with a bit of personal style—but despite their varied looks, they do have things in common: (1) They are all incredibly skinny. (2) They are all looking at me with "meanface." That's what Julie and I call it when a girl stares at you like you just stole her boyfriend. These girls have meanface down to a science.

Angela leads me into a room that has a wall of windows. The floors are concrete, and it looks like there was an art class in here earlier—there are little splatters of paint on the walls and easels in the corner. I see a rack of clothes hanging across from a folding bake-sale-style table, where two guys with glasses like Roger's sit. When they see Angela, one of them shrieks.

"Oh, Angie Angel! Is this *her*?" He turns to me and takes my hands, holding them out from my body and looking me up and down. "Doll, let's dress you up!" he says, dropping my arms and skipping over to the clothing rack. "I'm Mickey and that's Matt." He points to the other man at the desk, and I wonder how I'll ever tell them apart. They're both short and round, with red-apple cheeks and wavy black hair that looks slightly greasy. Though I guess Mickey's the one who talks. Matt hasn't said a word. But when I turn to smile at him at the table, a flash goes off. He snapped a Polaroid of me.

I look at Angela, but she just smiles and says, "Street-clothes shot, darling. Don't worry." Then she gestures to Mickey, so I go over to the clothes rack and he hands me a few outfits. "These!" he says, and points to one of those Asian screens in the corner. I'm guessing that's my dressing room, but it's facing the windows.

"Don't worry, sweets, no one'll see your tushie," says Mickey. He seems amused by my awkwardness, but not in an unkind way. "Panties on, bra off."

Angela's on the other side of the room on her cell phone, and I suddenly wish Mom were here. But I'm okay, I remember, and I try to channel that confident girl who sauntered around Bendel's yesterday. I smile and scoot behind the screen, starting to undress before I lose my nerve.

Each outfit is odder than the last—lots of flowing scarflike sleeves and skirts with little ties that leave lots of skin exposed. Mickey asks me to walk and spin, and then he takes a Polaroid of me in each outfit. While I'm walking, I try to remember that Angela said she liked the way I moved in the movie theater. So I picture myself on the dotted black carpet, hurrying to get Richard out of his office so a customer can see the manager. I'm not really relaxed, but then again, I wasn't exactly at ease the day Angela met me either.

When we say good-bye to Mickey and Matt—which is a series of kisses and shrieks—they take a few more Polaroids of me just in the sweater-and-jeans outfit (which, I have to say, is way conservative compared to the clothes they design). In some photos they want my glasses off, and Angela tells them I'll be getting contacts before the shows so my look will be versatile. This is news to me, but I stay quiet.

Out on the street, Angela flags down Mario and ushers me into the backseat. "You did wonderfully, Violet," she says. "Mario knows where to go next—you have six appointments today, so keep moving."

"Oh, are you not going to . . ."

"I've got a busy Sunday," Angela says. "I just wanted to get you through your virgin casting, but I can't hold your hand all day." Then she blows me a kiss and is gone, speed-walking down Greene Street, expertly sliding past a cyclist arguing with a guy in a suit and not even turning her head to look at a stand selling necklaces with chunky gem pendants.

I relax into the seat as Mario drives. That wasn't so bad. Mickey and Matt seemed to like me. Maybe today is going to be fun after all. If everyone's as friendly as the Tracetown guys, today will be a cakewalk. In Prada boots.

The next casting is not, in fact, easy as pie. Not only is dealing with the icy meanfaces of the models more difficult without

Angela leading me to the front of the line, but these designers are nothing like Mickey and Matt. I feel like I fell for a bait and switch— Angela brought me to the nicest designers ever and coddled me just before she threw me to the fashion wolves.

I'm pinned and prodded, shouted at and shoved. I'm told I'm "too Skeletor," "a little piggy," "kind of bland," and "crooked mouthed." One assistant even tells me she can see my "hedge," and I have no idea what she means until she motions to my bikini line. I turn bright red. Note to self: Go through with the wax. At my second and third appointments, I find myself on the brink of tears. I can feel my shoulders shrink in on themselves, and I can tell that I'm reverting back to the role of Violet Greenfield, reject high school student. It's not a good look.

Back in the car, Mario is encouraging, but I almost ask him to drive me back to Brooklyn. "I don't feel well," I lie. He raises his eyebrows at me in the rearview mirror.

"What's so scary about those fashion fools, Violet?" he asks.

"I don't know," I say. "They're experts who know I'm a loser who's not even very pretty—just tall."

"See, you're being negative," he says. "Ask me if I care if people think bald is sexy?" He laughs loudly and rubs his shiny head.

Despite Mario's optimism, I still expect myself to crumble at the next appointment. When I walk in, I see the same grim faces waiting in the hallway. I sit and put my head down, hunching over and trying not to make eye contact with anyone so I can't read on their faces that I don't belong there.

But I think about what Mario said, and I start to look around a little. These girls are all beautiful, but they look so sad. It's like they're characters in some kind of period drama or documentary about a hopeless, helpless people. The whole thing strikes me as absurd, since as glamorous models in New York City they're the envy of so many other girls, yet none of them cracks a smile.

I sit next to a beautiful girl who looks about fourteen. She has huge eyes and a really big head. Well, at first I think she has a big head, but then I realize that's because her body is teensy. I begin to wonder if my head looks oversized—the lollipop-on-a-stick look isn't so hot—and she catches me studying her face.

"Hi," she says softly. When she smiles, she looks much less terrifying.

"Hi," I say, hugging my knees in tightly.

"Nice boots," she says. "Did you do a Prada shoot?"

"Oh, no," I say, looking down at my leather-clad toes. "They're just, um, a gift." I wasn't ready to explain that Angela kind of bought them for me. If she even did.

"Aha!" says Lollipop. "Someone's got a sweet sugar daddy!"

I stare at her for a minute, shocked. Is she old enough to be talking like that? Before I can even respond, she stands up, smiles, and heads into the casting room. All I can do is laugh a little to let out my tension. It actually helps, and although people around me stare as I giggle softly to myself, I feel loosened up, and I don't mind them looking.

When the bookings lady gazes at me straight on and tells me I'm "mealy eyed," I find myself wanting to write down the insult so I can remember it for Roger and Julie. I imagine us laughing hysterically back in my room about the adventurous, exciting, but ultimately un-successful experiment of Violet Greenfield, Top Model. And the more psyched I get about sharing all of this with my friends, the less seriously I take these comical people with foreign-sounding names and affected accents. Between the last few castings, I can't wait to get back to the car to tell Mario what the designers said to me and how the other models acted. He has a big, open guffaw of a laugh, and I find myself having fits of hysteria in the backseat—this whole world is completely amusing.

I'm sure Angela will be furious, but at my last casting I ask if I can have one of my own Polaroids. I want Julie to put it in the extensive scrapbook she's sure to put together after senior year is over.

"This film is like a dollar a shot," says the annoyed assistant, who has way too much product in his hair. It reminds me of Cameron Diaz in *There's Something About Mary*—that scene where her hair is sticking straight up after she mistakes Ben Stiller's, um, love juice for gel.

"Oh, I can pay," I say, pulling a dollar from my wallet and snatching the photo from his hands. He smiles then, and I head for the door.

"Violet!" he yells. Up until that point I had no idea he knew my name—I figured I was just another nameless, faceless potential clothes hanger for his boss. I turn and look over my shoulder, and he snaps one more Polaroid. "Money," he says.

I wink and head out the door.

Mario really enjoys that story, and he's a fan of the Polaroid too. When he drops me off in Brooklyn, I shake his hand and say good-bye.

"I'll see you in a couple of weeks, Violet," he says.

"Oh, no, Mario," I say. "I don't think I'll be back up here. I totally blew those castings—I had no idea what I was doing."

"Girl, you did better than you think," says Mario, as I open the door. "I'll be seeing you."

Aunt Rita is sitting in the overstuffed chair of the front room, humming. She's reading the *New York Times* at the same time, which sort of impresses me.

"Hey, kid," she says. "Want some dinner?"

She starts toward the kitchen when Mom comes rushing down the stairs. "Violet! Is that you? How did it go?"

"Oh, it wasn't that great," I say, suddenly feeling lame about myself. Maybe I should have taken everything more seriously today.

"Let her sit down and get a bite, Jane," says Rita. "We can hear all about those Snooty McSnoots over dinner." She catches my eye and smiles.

Mom looks worried. "Oh, dear, didn't you do well? With all that money Angela spent on you?"

I'm about to explain to Mom that I'm just not like those other girls who are successful models. I don't want to wait in dark hallways and keep a mean face on; I don't want to have to pretend I can't hear what the designers are saying when they discuss my knees and my "surly little toes" right in front of me. I get enough abuse from my own inner voice. I remember the moment when I took the Polaroid—probably the biggest faux pas a "new model" made all day—and it makes me smile.

But I don't get to tell Mom about any of that because my cell phone rings.

"Victorious Violet!"

"Hi, Angela," I say quietly. She must not have heard about the day yet. I wonder how long it takes designers to draw a big X across my Polaroids and send them back to Tryst. I start to worry about whether I'll be able to keep the boots. I wore them all day, so I don't think Bendel's will take them back, right?

"Four shows," she says.

"Huh?"

"You booked four shows." Then she pauses, maybe to let it sink in, but I still don't respond. I'm not sure if I've heard her correctly. Maybe she said, "You owe me four thousand dollars for those freaking boots."

"Violet, this is huge!" she shrieks. "They loved your raw act and your unpolished walk, just like I knew they would. Four shows is more than Veronica Trask booked on her cherry castings four years ago."

I start to smile doofily into the phone. Veronica Trask is one of those models who gets to be on the cover of teen magazines even though most only use celebrities these days—just because she's that famous.

"I'll need to talk to your mother," continues Angela. "Of course you'll just be making scale—only a hundred and fifty an hour at first, but we'll bump you up soon. I also want to discuss a possible move to our model apartment—once you do the shows you can start booking campaigns and making a real name for yourself."

I can't really take in what Angela is saying—a hundred and fifty dollars an hour?!—but she lets me go and says she'll call us later this week. When I tell Mom and Rita that I booked some shows, Mom hugs me and acts thrilled. Now it's Rita who has a worried look, but she starts humming again as she prepares mac and cheese for us.

Mom and I sit in front of the evening news, but I'm not paying attention. I'm thinking about how I can't wait to see the look on Shelly Ryan's face when she hears about my real-life runway adventure, which is just about to start.

ten

I miss morning classes on Monday because our flight gets in at ten A.M., but I call Julie and Roger to tell them that I'll be in by lunch. I ask them to meet me in the newspaper office, since I'm sure Julie will be there anyway. I have *got* to tell them about everything that's happening.

I wore my boots on the plane from LaGuardia, but when I landed in Raleigh, they felt silly. I changed in the car—back to Converse and my regular (not skinny) jeans. And yes, a long-torso tank top. I even pull my hair back into a ponytail so it won't look too different. I do allow myself the new glasses, though—those I really love.

When I walk into the newspaper office, Julie is writing a to-do list for the staff on a whiteboard. Roger is staring at one of the over-sized monitors, snickering.

"What's up?" I ask.

"Oh, nothing," says Roger, not looking up. "Just scrolling

through the photo options for the front page of the sports section this week. Your friend Brian has more than one bad side."

I look at the screen and see Brian Radcliff making, I'll admit it, a fairly unattractive face on the football field. Sometimes Roger is so immature.

Julie finishes the list and turns around, running over to give me a hug. "Your glasses!" she says. Then Roger takes an interest and lifts his apathetic head. "Cool!" he says. "Did you get those in Williamsburg?"

"Um, no," I say. "I just thought they were cute."

"And your hair!" says Julie. "Take it down, Violet. Did you get it highlighted?"

"I believe the term is *lowlights*," I say, enjoying this attention from my friends. "But yeah, I kind of had a mini-makeover in New York."

"Well, you look smashing, darling," Roger says in a fake accent that sounds scarily like Angela's actual voice.

"How's Rita?" Julie asks. I suddenly remember that I forgot to go to H&M for her, and I feel a little guilty. But I'm hoping my news will make up for it.

"She's the same," I say, sitting down at the end of the long staff-meeting table. "Still weird, still wielding mud." I smile and look at my two best friends, who are grinning back at me expectantly. They know I wouldn't ask them to meet me at lunch just for haircut approval and a recap of the weekend. Besides, Julie called me twice— and Roger once—while I was in New York, and I didn't return their calls. I didn't even get the messages until last night because I was in such another world. And Rita's got no Internet access, so my IM name is collecting dust. They're aware that something's up.

"So, Miss Greenfield. Why have you gathered us here today?" asks Roger. "It wasn't just so we could fawn over your lowlights, was it? I didn't bring a lunch, so if you talk fast we might be able to book to Wendy's for the dollar menu before the bell."

"Is this about pot smoking?" asks Julie. "Because I can see you feeling all awkward and serious and guilty if you lit up with Aunt Rita, but Roger and I really won't care, Violet. Promise."

"I'll care!" shouts Roger, standing up for dramatic effect. "Friends are my antidrug!"

"Shut up, Roger," I say, laughing. "I just had something to tell you guys." I've thought about how to tell Julie and Roger my news in a way that will make them (a) know immediately that I'm not kidding, (b) not be mean or judgmental about it, and (c) not be offended that I didn't tell them sooner. I figure going chronologically is easiest, so I start with last weekend at the movie theater when I met Angela. I explain how I wasn't really sure anything was real or going to happen, but then how this weekend in New York, I actually got a makeover from Tryst (I leave out the clothes part because I don't want Roger to call me a shallow consumer, and Julie will appreciate it more with the visual aid of my Prada boots). And I tell them how Angela set up meetings with these designers and how I'm actually going to be a runway model in a couple of weeks. I'm not sure how much detail to include, so it all spills out in about two minutes. I figure we can get into the ridiculous, hilarious parts later, after the roller-skating-giraffe-turns-model part sinks in. Judging by their open but silent mouths, they need a few more minutes.

Julie looks over at Roger and I think she realizes that both of their jaws are agape, so she slams hers shut and smiles. "Violet! That's amazing!" she says. "I mean, it's sort of annoying that you didn't tell us sooner—we *are* your best friends—but I'm happy for you. Can we come see your debut in New York?"

"Oh, thanks, Jules," I say, relieved. "I knew you'd be excited. And wait till I show you the boots I got—leather, P-R-A-D-A!"

"What am I, a toddler with no language skills?" says Roger, standing up from the table. At first I think he's going to storm out—he looks kind of tense—but then he leans over to hug me. "I always knew you were gorgeous, kid," he says in his Humphrey Bogart voice. "Sounds like the rest of the world is about to find out too." Then he straightens up and says, "So who wants Wendy's?"

"I'll go," I say. "Jules?" She's already back at the whiteboard, poised to add more to the to-do list.

"Oh, no," she says. "You guys go. I've got to keep working on this—it's my day to lead the staff meeting." It seems bizarre that my friends don't have a hundred questions about what my weekend was like, who the other models were, which inane expressions Angela employs. Usually Julie and Roger are in it for the details, if only so they can mock with more precision. But neither one of them seems particularly interested. Maybe I'm being self-absorbed and they're just busy. I shrug and make a mental vow not to talk about Tryst at Wendy's—I'll ask lots of questions about what went on here this weekend so I don't seem narcissistic. Then I grab my bag and run after Roger, who's already out the door.

For the rest of the day at school, I feel deflated. Roger didn't bring up my news at all during lunch, but he did make a couple of jokes about the average IQ of the supermodel and tried to engage me in some hearty ridiculing of Tyra Banks's talk show.

On the drive home, I feel less like Violet Greenfield, Polaroid-stealing IT girl, and more like Violet Greenfield, local loser. I thought your friends were supposed to build you up, but Julie and Roger barely talk to me in the car—they yammer on about how great *SNL* was this weekend (as if I believe that).

At home, Dad has made a cake. He even tried to draw a runway on it, and there's one of those tiny generic-brand Barbie-style dolls on top. I appreciate Dad's baked goods, but I also see them for what they are: an excuse to extend the dinner-table conversation. Mom is pretty swept up in the Tryst project—especially since we learned I'll get a couple thousand dollars for each runway show I booked—but Dad still has some major reservations. Angela apparently called Mom at work today and laid out a plan for me to miss school during Fashion Week. Dad wants me to talk to all of my teachers and outline a schedule for making up work, which is fine. I mean, missing a week of school during my senior year when I already have practically enough credits to graduate is not a big deal. I tell Dad how I have my UNC application ready so I can be considered for early admission—then I'll at least be into my safety school. In fact, the whole conversation goes pretty smoothly.

It's not until Mom's clearing the cake plates that I realize Jake has hardly said a word to me since I've been home. I look at him and smile, trying to catch his gaze, but he pops up from his chair. "Are we done here?" he asks Dad, who nods. Then he bounds up the stairs. I look at Dad to see if he noticed Jake's odd behavior, but Dad just starts repeating how I really do need to make sure my academics are in order before I leave for New York. I swear he's said this at least four times.

"I will, Dad, okay?" Then I use Jake's line: "Are we done here?"

Dad smirks. "Yes, smarty pants, we're done." I smile at him and head to my room, where I put on Norah Jones because—after the nonreaction from Julie and Roger, plus my parents' nagging and Jake's silent treatment—I'm feeling a little angsty.

Over the next couple of weeks, things kind of go back to normal at school. I finally get contacts, at Angela's insistence, but it doesn't seem like many people even notice. I wear my glasses most of the time anyway—partly because I do really like the frames, and partly because it still takes me twenty minutes to get my contacts in, and it hurts a little. The thrill of my new haircut wears off, and Shelly Ryan doesn't say a word to me about the mall runway show. In fact, the BK girls haven't talked to me at all lately. Part of me wants them to find out about Tryst, but I don't want to be the one to tell them—that's lame. I want people at school to be buzzing with the news of my modeling career. But I guess I haven't really got one. Yet.

I haven't talked to anyone besides Roger and Julie about Fashion Week—and even my two best friends seem not to care. I notice that when I bring up anything model-related with Roger and Julie, they act like freaks. Roger behaves as I'd expect, really—he makes snide comments about the fashion world and all its excesses, keeps tabs on what I eat each day to make sure I'm not skimping on meals, and reminds me to try not to grow up to be Janice Dickinson. I guess it's really Julie who's disappointing me. She says she's happy for me, and excited, but lately talking to her is like talking to the Bee's Knees girls—there's an emptiness to her words. For the first time in our friendship, it seems like she's, well, faking it.

Even the day she came over to do homework and I showed her the Prada boots, she held them for a minute and then just went back to an overly intense stare at her calculus book. I know she's really into her grades right now because it's the last semester that's going to count for her college applications, but I'm annoyed that she isn't excited for me.

One Saturday night, I'm working the ticket box at the movie theater. There's a steady stream of customers, but it's not crazy busy so I open the door to talk to Benny, a college student who's working concession. It's so easy to spill your life to co-workers here. It's like if they don't go to your high school, they barely exist on the same planet.

"It's hard to concentrate in class," I say, explaining to Benny how I daydream about my next trip to New York—half excited, half terrified.

Richard comes out of his office as the stream of customers slows. Ever since I told theater people about the Tryst stuff, Richard has been swearing up and down that he taught me everything I know about "working the runway," and now he interrupts me and Benny. "Oh, silly little flower," he says. Richard takes any opportunity to employ a new nickname. "What are you worried about class for? You are going to make millions with our signature walk! And then you'll split the money with me, your mentor. Oh, please tell André Leon Talley that we'd be good together—I know we would."

I don't even know what he's talking about, so I ignore him and continue talking to Benny. Eventually, Richard finds an audience in Chelsea, a new girl who's working the second concession area. I'm glad he's gone because I feel like Benny's pretty quiet unless you get him one-on-one. He's a stoner type who doesn't say much, but when he does, wise things come out of his mouth. When I get to the part about how Julie and Roger are acting strange, he says, "Classic jealousy."

"Nah," I say. They both have so much going for them—I just can't picture them begrudging me this one moment of excitement in my boring little life.

"They don't mean to be jealous, dude," Benny says. "It sounds like—from the way you've said they're acting—they're actually, like, trying to fight it." He takes a straw from the dispenser and starts to twist each end tightly around his index fingers.

"I don't know . . ." I say.

"Well, Julie's definitely wearing a fake perma-grin. And she's like a big overachiever, so anything you do that she doesn't is going to make her feel totally insecure. Roger, though, I can't really figure out. Maybe he has a crush on you and doesn't want you getting eyed by other guys?"

I have to laugh out loud then, and I nearly spit the Sprite I've been drinking. "Um, I don't think so," I say. "At least about the Roger part. I think he's just being snarky." I consider what Benny said for a minute, crushing up the ice in the bottom of my cup. "You may have a point about Julie. But what should I do? I'm not going to give up Fashion Week just because she can't do it too."

"You gotta talk to her," says Benny. Then he holds out the air-filled straw bubble he's tightened between his hands. With a flick of my finger, I break it and we both smile at the satisfying *SMACK!* it makes.

When I get home, I log on to IM and see if Julie's on. Her screen name is "Diane Sawyer," which she says is a joke, but Roger and I have agreed that we think she's totally serious.

"Whatcha doin?" I IM. I kind of want her to come over, but I'm scared to ask. I normally feel completely secure around Julie and totally insecure with the rest of the planet, but lately it's like my worlds have switched. I'm starting to feel more confident around *other* people. Benny said he liked my hair, and he never notices anything (partially because he hardly looks up from the candy counter). And even though no one really knows about Tryst yet at school and I'm still just the Jolly Green Giant, I walk around feeling like I have this secret—that I know that there's something special about me. God, that sounds lame, but it's actually how I feel. And I think it might even be helping my posture.

It takes Julie a few minutes to answer me, which means either she's busy being superstudent or she just wants to seem like she doesn't have time for me. "Work," she writes. Not exactly an invitation to chat from Diane Sawyer.

"Oh, ok," I type. But then I erase it. If I can't be real with Julie, how will I ever be real with anyone? "Hmm . . . well, can we talk?" I say, hitting Enter before I can overthink it.

"About what?" is her reply. The girl doesn't give an inch.

"I'm calling you," is all I write. Then I pick up my cell and flop down on my bed.

"Hey," I say. And after we get past all the blah, blah about our days and she tells me about the stories she's working on for newspaper and I tell her about how the new girl at the theater is still amused by Richard's antics, I say, "So, I'm feeling like you're acting distant lately." And then the line goes quiet.

When Julie gets quiet, she's admitting guilt. If she weren't being distant, she would have a hundred and one reasons to explain how she's busy and she loves me and she'll make it up to me with an ice cream, *Grease*, *Grease 2* party next weekend. Because it's not like I've never said this to her. She gets busy and I feel alone and eventually I speak up. But this time, it's different. And her silence proves it.

"Violet," she says. "I'm going to tell you something, but it's hard for me to say, okay?" And that's when I know that Benny is right. Julie—the newspaper editor, the flit-between-social-groups hallway butterfly, my sweet and petite best friend who has an incredible sense of style—is jealous. Of me.

"I know it's not mind-blowing," she continues, "but I am jealous. Who wouldn't be? Violet, you get to go to New York City and possibly become, like, the next Gemma Ward! You get a makeover and contacts and a chauffeur. And fucking PRADA BOOTS!" She screams that last part, and I can't help but smile a little because now she's back to being herself. She laughs then, and we dissolve into a fit of laughter. "When I saw those things I nearly threw them across the room, I was so jealous!" she says, still giggling, so I know things are going to be cool between us.

"I KNEW they impressed you more than you let on," I say.

"Duh!" she shouts. Then her voice gets soft again. "Look, I'm really sorry. I didn't know how to handle the news when you sprung it on us Monday, and I've kind of been working through things this week, talking to my life coach . . ."

"Remember—you are beautiful and confident and wise," I tease.

"Oh, shut up!" she says, but I can tell by her tone that she's still smiling. "I really am sorry, though. I promise to be more supportive— seriously."

"Thanks," I say. "And you know, maybe you can come up to New York and meet Mario. I don't think he has a prom date yet."

"Ha-ha, Greenfield. I'm already working on that, actually."

"Oh, really, with whom?"

"You'll see," Julie says. And I don't even care that she's being elusive. I'm just glad to have her on my side again.

eleven

Two weeks later, I'm on another plane to New York City—this time without Mom, who has to work and is kind of frantic about me going alone, but I'm actually glad to be solo. Roger hasn't stopped sniping about models being one-brain-celled clothes hangers, but Julie has been great these last few days. She helped me shop for a few key "model pieces," which she says include slouchy shirts and dresses to pair with my skinny jeans and ballet flats. Julie even found me a pair of oversized sunglasses at Time After Time, our local vintage store, so I feel semi–rock-starish at check-in. I have to admit that when I board the plane in Raleigh this time, I see a few heads turn to look my way.

Mom gave me cab money because Rita says she's not coming to the airport for me again. I'm hoping she's going to be cool about me staying with her for the next ten days. And by "be cool" I mean I hope she just kind of stays in her own space. Mom asked her to take care of me, but Rita just laughed and said I could take care of myself, but yes, I could sleep in the downstairs room. That made Mom even more nervous, but I took it as a good sign.

When I arrive in Brooklyn, no one hears me knocking for a while. I call Rita on my cell but there's no answer. I'm not sure what to do, so I drop my bags and sit on the stoop, pulling out the issue of *Us Weekly* that I bought for the plane. I'm almost done with it—I just have to read the Fashion Police section in the back, which is my least favorite. I page through the celebrity gossip a few times, and the sun starts to beat down a bit on my shoulders, making them pink and darkening my light freckles. I can feel beads of sweat forming on my forehead, and I wonder if I should just go to a coffee shop or something, but then Rita opens the door. She's wearing an off-white apron covered in clay over her T-shirt and sweats, and she seems surprised to see me.

"Oh, Violet! Is today Wednesday?" she says. "Where did the week get away to? Well, come on inside. I've got my boys out back, but they're friendly."

I walk in and head downstairs to drop off my suitcase. Rita follows me and steps outside to the garden. "Violet! Come out here and meet the first-grade potters!"

In the backyard, a group of five six-year-old boys are huddled around Rita's two picnic tables, playing with clay. "My after-school ceramics class," she says. "Boys, meet Violet, my niece."

The kids smile politely and then go back to molding their clay into lopsided bowls and round-ball animal shapes. One boy keeps staring at me, though, and I start to feel weird, like he's going to say something mean that only little kids say because they don't yet know how to be polite—and they're super honest. I expect him to ask me just how tall I am, or how much I weigh, or whether I'm like that girl Alice who went down the bathtub drain in that horrible children's song (yes, I actually had a kid I babysat for ask me if I was related to "Alice, with legs like toothpicks and a neck like a giraffe").

"Are you a movie star?" he asks instead, and I'm taken aback.

"That's my Daniel," says Rita, mussing his hair. "Always a charmer with the ladies." Daniel is still staring at me, so I smile.

"No, Daniel," I reply. "Just a regular girl. Why do you ask?"

"You're pretty as a movie star," he says, then giggles and looks back to his clay. And I feel like that is the nicest thing anyone's said to me in a long time.

At dinner that night, Rita orders Chinese food. "I was just cooking to impress your mom," she says, letting out a big laugh. She's so strange. Like Mom was going to be impressed by canned soup and toast? But I'm glad she's not trying to impress me—and besides, I'd rather eat takeout anyway.

I order sesame chicken and Rita gets beef barbecue. When she tells me she's glad to see I'm eating heartily and not bowing to the pressures of the modeling world, I decide to leave half of my dinner untouched. Maybe I should be worried about that—and sesame chicken isn't exactly salad.

We watch TV—luckily she's into reality shows, which are my favorites too—and Rita doesn't even ask me about Fashion Week or what my schedule is like. She yawns and stretches around eleven P.M. "Phew! I'm tuckered out," she says, getting up from the couch where we've been glued since the delivery guy came around seven. "I'm hitting the hay. Good night, Violet."

And then I'm alone, with no parents or Rita or bedtime or plan. I think about how if I were a more exciting person, I'd sneak out and go into Manhattan to go to Bungalow 8 or My Place or one of the other clubs I read about in *Us Weekly* today. But I just go to bed instead, because I'm pretty tired. And, who am I kidding—I'm no velvet-rope breaker. Yet.

*   *   *

The next day, Rita's gone before I wake up. There's a note on the table that says, "Farmer's market—back at noon. R." but it's already eleven A.M., and I have to get going. Angela's call woke me up (thank goodness), and I tried to sound bright-eyed—I even cleared my throat and practiced talking before I actually answered the phone—but she knew I was still sleeping. "Violet on Valium," she said, "Mario will be there at eleven-thirty to get you, dear. You've got a fitting and a rehearsal at noon." Then she was gone.

When I hear Mario's honk, I shovel the last bits of sesame chicken leftovers into my mouth, grab my bag, and race to the car. Mario is all smiles, so he doesn't even need to say "I told you so"—I can tell we're both happy that I booked a few shows.

"Where to, V?" he asks. "Prada? Marc Jacobs?" I laugh and he drives toward Soho. He probably knows my schedule better than I do, but I remember that my first fitting is at Tracetown with Mickey and Matt, which is good because they were the nicest to me during castings. All the shows I booked are for relatively new designers, so it's not like I'm walking for Chanel, but I'm actually glad—working with a legendary brand would be so scary. I talk about that with Mario as we drive, and he tells me that people don't say "brand," they say "house," as in "The House of Versace." I have so much to learn. I decide to stay silent during my fitting—I don't want to sound like a bumpkin.

As we pull up to Mickey and Matt's studio, I almost miss having Mom on this trip. I feel like a little girl, wishing she'd walk in with me and hold my hand the way she used to do when I went to the pediatrician. Not that this is anything like a doctor's appointment, but I am fighting a familiar sense of dread in my stomach that's very much like the feeling I'd get on a shot-and-lollipop afternoon.

Mario must see me biting my nails as I exit the car, because he yells out the window to me as I start to walk into Tracetown's building. "Hey, V!" he shouts. "Pretty as a movie star!" And even though

I don't believe in much beyond my astrologyzone.com horoscope, I take that as a good sign.

The fittings aren't bad. The clothes are fussed over and fiddled with and fingered, but I don't have to do or say much, and I start to think Roger was right—if not about the one-brain-cell part then at least about the clothes-hanger thing. It's like I'm a mannequin with no feelings. Still, I'm starting to view these dusty design studios as sort of glamorous with their faded mirrors and worn dress forms. The first part of the day goes by in a flash, and soon I'm headed for Bryant Park, an outdoor space in midtown Manhattan where the fashion tents are set up, for a rehearsal.

In the car on the way there, I realize that I haven't eaten since the cold sesame chicken. Mario points to the backseat pocket, where there's a fiber bar and a bottle of water—um, yuck. "Can we stop for pizza?" I ask. "I swear I won't spill." He pulls over, laughing, and I jump out and grab a pepperoni slice. Though he's amused, Mario won't let me eat in the car, so I stand on the sidewalk, shove the pizza into my mouth, and hurry back into the backseat.

We get to Bryant Park just in time. I pause for a minute to take in the expansive space between huge skyscrapers, the white tents that seem to be their own city in the middle of a swath of grass, the frantic fashion types running around with Bluetooth headsets and Blackberrys. I see Angela flapping a clipboard at me as I wave good-bye to Mario. Does he really just sit and wait for me all day—or does he jet off to meet his wife for lunch and then come back so I never know he was gone? I wonder which other models he drives around when I'm not here. It seems like an odd job, but he says he gets a lot of reading done and has three days off each week to hang out with Linda and their four-year-old daughter, Lucia. I guess it's not so bad.

"Viva la Violet!" Angela says, holding out her arms to me. This time I know it's not a welcome sign for "hug" but rather a "stay at arms length, please" sign for air kissing. I'm learning.

"Let's get you right into the tent," she says, rushing off toward the center of the lawn and somehow balancing on the balls of her feet so that her heels don't sink into the grass. Thank goodness I got these ballet flats. "Nice dress," she says, as she glances back, and I can't tell if she's serious. It's one of the dresses Julie picked out for me—baby-doll with a light blue toile print—and I decide that I'll tell Julie it got a fashionista compliment, even if Angela was being facetious.

"I can't be with you all night, darling V, so you're going to be going around with Veronica—you booked some of the same shows," says Angela. "My two Vs!"

I suck in my breath. Veronica Trask is playing big sister to *me*? She'll see right through me. She'll know I'm a gawky geek from the Carolinas who has no business being in the fashion capital of the country—maybe the world. And then I see her, staring at me from behind a dressing screen. Steely brown eyes, arched brows and a straight, Roman nose. Her lips are covered by the top of the screen—like that neighbor Wilson on *Home Improvement*—but I think I detect a hint of a smile playing on her face. And it isn't a nice one.

"Violet, I presume." Veronica steps out from behind her dressing screen in a full-length, golden gown with what must be ten layers of white tulle filling out the skirt. She looks like a brown-eyed, brunette version of Cinderella, until she pulls me close to whisper in my ear, "You're going to fall flat on your pasty, freckled face." Make that a wicked stepsister.

My eyes are enlarged and frozen as she leans back from me, but when I look at her face she's smiling, as if she's just told me she's so glad we're going to be very best friends.

"Be good, girls," says Angela. "Violet, remember not to smile—

this isn't a beauty pageant, it's a fashion show. And use your natural walk—that's what they love, so don't be affected. I've got to check on Jakele now." And then she's gone and I'm alone with Shelly Ryan to the Infinite Power.

"Your clothes are over there," she says, pointing to a folding metal chair with piles of fabric strewn around it. "You have two changes, so make sure they fit, and get ready to rehearse the order."

Veronica starts to undress as Mickey rushes in. "Girls! Have you seen Matt? I can't find him and we have to start the—aaahhh!" A high-pitched shriek punctuates his question as he looks over to my area of the dressing room. "Who lumped these clothes here? Violet? You cannot do that—they must stay on the racks or on you—never, never on the floor!"

"Oh, but I . . ." I start to explain, but—surprise—someone interrupts.

"I tried to tell her, Mickey," says Veronica, smiling. "Poor thing is just not used to nice clothes. It's not her fault that Target's designer series is as close to couture as she's seen."

Mickey rolls his eyes and begins to hang my clothes on the rack. "I didn't mean to . . ." I start, trying to fight the quiver in my voice.

"It's fine, Violet," he says, still breathing hard. "You're new, you're new." It's almost like he's trying to talk himself out of punishing me for something I didn't even do. And I want to explain that it was Veronica who dumped the clothes like that, how I would never treat his designs that way. But all I can do is fight back tears—and even that isn't working well. "Now get dressed!" yells Mickey, as he walks outside. "Rehearsal in five!"

Veronica looks over innocently, as if she hasn't just completely sabotaged me. "Oh, Violet," she says softly. "Is it that easy, teardrop?"

I look back at her, still silent, unsure of how to respond. "By the way," she adds in a saccharine voice, "You might want to pop a breath mint after pizza."

Then she pulls on the purple flowing tea-length dress she's wearing for her first walk and heads out of the tent. And I put my head down on the makeup counter and cry, thinking it's a good thing I'm not wearing mascara yet.

By the time we line up for rehearsal, I've at least gotten my puffy eyes down. Not that any of the other models are paying the slightest bit of attention to me. In fact, they seem to move around each other like robots who've never experienced human interaction. To be fair, a lot of them seem to be from other countries, so maybe they just don't speak English.

I'm in a line, waiting to walk out into the blinding lights of Fashion Week (well, Fashion Week Rehearsal, anyway), when I realize that I've never before walked an actual runway. I've just walked around a room for people. Or on a theater carpet for Angela. What if it's really narrow and I plummet off the side? Maybe the floor is slippery. And I'm still not very good at walking in heels, though Julie and I did practice that with her three-inch sophomore-winter-formal shoes the night before I left (not that that session inspired confidence, since I fell twice).

A few sharp shoulders jostle me, and no one says "sorry" or "excuse me," but I'm getting used to this model code of silence. And judging by the icy, empty stares on these girls, I might be better off just coexisting with them and not actually interacting. Interacting is what Veronica and I did earlier, I guess, and I'm not up for any more of that.

As the girl in front of me walks onto the stage, I start to peek around the curtain to see how she walks and turns, in hopes that I can learn something in, oh, the next thirty seconds. "Whoa—don't do that!" a voice behind me whisper-yells. "They'll see you poking round!" A striking redhead is just behind me, and judging by her accent, she's from Australia. She's smiling at my mistake, but not in an unkind way, and I make a mental note to find out who she is. But there's no time to even thank her for saving me from curtain-peeking humiliation because it's suddenly my turn to get out on the runway.

I walk into the blinding lights and try to remember the advice Angela gave me: don't smile, natural walk. The not-smiling part is easy because I'm scared shitless, and although I'm not sure I'm wearing that dead-eyed, sour-mouthed face that everyone else seems to be sporting around here, I'm most definitely not smiling. The walking part is harder, mainly because I'm in boots with major heels and I've got a piecey, flowing Tracetown dress milling about my legs and threatening to trip me at any moment. I'm kind of in a blind panic, but I don't fall and no one seems to gasp in horror at my gawky ugliness, so that's a positive. I also notice that my "audience" is Angela and Mickey, along with a couple of models milling about who aren't really watching. There's a janitor in the corner who's leaning on his broom and looking bored to death.

When I get backstage I have to quickly change into my second Tracetown outfit—black cotton shorts and a blue-and-multicolored-polka-dot button top with lace-up-the-leg sandals. The shoes are the hardest part, but Mickey gave me a tutorial in how to lace them, and apparently at the real show we'll have people backstage helping us get dressed. I manage to tie something together and hope it doesn't look too sloppy. Then I step out again and enter that state-of-fear walk. This time it's easier because the sandals, though high, have a wedge heel that's better for my balance.

Then I'm done. I've pulled off my first fashion show rehearsal!

Unfortunately, I have to do three more before I'm allowed to fall back into Mario's car and go back to Rita's. At the end of it all, I'm exhausted, and it isn't just from the walking and the quick changes.

"No one talked to me, Mario," I say, as I finally get to rest my head on the leather seats and head to Brooklyn. "Everyone just looked really mean." I think about the redheaded Australian girl and give her a mental exception. I didn't see her after the first show, though, so there was no opportunity to talk to her and determine whether she's normal. Man, I need Julie here.

"It's work, Violet," says Mario. "They do a job, they leave."

But isn't it supposed to be fun and dazzling and laughter-filled backstage? "I guess," I say, not wanting to sound naïve, even with Mario. "I just thought it would be . . ."

"More glamorous?" Mario asks with a smile.

"Yeah," I say, leaning back against the seat. "I'm being stupid."

"Nah, Violet, you're being real," he says. "And you'll find some friends here. Don't you worry."

"Oh, it's okay," I say. "It's just a week so I don't even really need to make friends here. I guess I just hoped everyone would be friend*ly* and not, well, like stoic aliens."

"Ha-ha," Mario's guffaw makes me smile. "You'll have some stories for Aunt Rita, though, V."

Oh my God! *Aunt Rita!* I didn't get to leave her a note or call her all day! I check my phone—three missed calls: Julie, Mom, Julie. I wonder if Rita even has my cell number. She must be pacing the floors with worry—it's eleven P.M.

When I get to the house, though, the lights are off and Rita's nowhere to be found. I creep upstairs to her room and find her fast asleep. Like she wasn't concerned at all. Huh. I wonder if I should feel happy about that or offended.

Downstairs in my Raggedy Ann room, I think about the day and how I'll re-create it for Julie and Roger when I get home. I wish I could take pictures of these girls' faces to show the unhappy frowns and pouty eyes they wear—even when they're not on the runway. The Australian girl seemed kind of bubbly, though. I got to see her start her walk since she was directly behind me, and there was definitely a bounce in her step. One of the makeup guys told me she's only eighteen—but she's got tons of experience. "Her first runway show was four years ago and, honey, that girl is fierce!" he said. And, of course, Veronica stands out completely with her signature, strong-legged march, but she's a superstar—and she always gets to end the show by walking out with the designer and holding hands. That's the mark of a real celebrity model. Well, at least I didn't stick out like I was afraid I would. But do I really fit in with all those toothpick-thin, dreary-faced girls? Is that who I am? Is that who I want to be here?

twelve

The next morning Aunt Rita's in the kitchen, humming as usual. "Fruit!" she chirps, setting down an oversized bowl filled with melons and yogurt and granola. I realize that I'm starving—and so glad Rita went to the farmer's market yesterday so there's at least something in the house.

"So today is opening day?" asks Rita, sitting down with me at the table.

"Yup," I say, wondering if fashion people would call it "opening day"—sounds more like a horse-racing term or something.

"Fantastic!" says Rita. And then she just opens the newspaper and starts reading while she crunches on her hippie food. She doesn't even ask me how yesterday went or if I'm nervous about— *hello!*—walking in New York Fashion Week.

I finish my food and put the bowl in the sink. If Rita's not interested, I'm not interested in sharing. I call Julie, but she's at school and doesn't answer. I consider trying Mom, but talking to her would probably just put me more on edge. I'm on my own.

I don't think Rita even notices when I leave the house—she's already out back working on her giant bowls or animal sculptures or whatever potters do—but I do write a note just in case, telling her I have one show tonight and I'll be back not too late, eleven P.M. or so. I also leave my cell phone number, in case she wants to check in or anything.

Backstage at the tents, it's way more hectic than yesterday. There are hair people, makeup people, assistants to help us get dressed. I see mirrors hung from precarious poles, piles of clothing, designer bags heaped in the corner of the tent and, of course, the girls from last night—still frowning, but now with an air of panic about them.

My instinct is to go hide in the corner, which is exactly what I do, even though some inner voice is telling me that I should push in and assert the fact that I have a right to be here. I see Veronica doing just that in the center mirror—four makeup and hair people buzzing around her—and it makes me jealous. Not envious that she's Veronica Trask or that she has flawless, sun-kissed skin and Herbal-Essence-commercial-worthy hair. But just in awe of her self-confidence and of the way she owns everything around her effortlessly. It's the same way Shelly Ryan—even though she's not nearly as pretty as Veronica—captivates the school. Even people who hate her (i.e., me, at least in theory and as far as Julie and Roger know), also love her in some way. I find myself watching Veronica and wondering how to get that essence of power. Hopefully without the side order of bitchy behavior.

Of course, it's a little hard to conjure power and glory when you're shoved behind a corner tent flap to change, which is the spot I've chosen for myself. I pull my first outfit off the rack and start to undress. A tiny woman in pinstriped socks and suspenders, wearing cat's-eye glasses and totally pulling off bright red dreadlocks, comes over to me with pins in her mouth.

"Violet, right?" she asks, smiling and somehow still holding those pins tightly between her lips.

I nod.

"I'm Sandy. Okay, let's get you ready," she says, grabbing my dress and pulling it down over my hips. In two minutes (as opposed to the ten it took me yesterday to line up seams and make sure everything was falling right), I'm snuggled perfectly into the dress.

"Makeup, Henry!" Sandy the sock lady yells, and then she's gone, replaced by a round Asian man with flamboyant hands.

"Violet Greenfield," he says, grinning widely. "Girl, I've heard about you." Then he whisks me into a chair in front of a crooked mirror and starts pulling brushes and powders out of his black, lipstick-stained apron. "Good bones, green eyes, and oooh, those freckles!"

Henry chatters on, talking about the show and the clothes and who'll be in the audience—like editors from every magazine I've ever read, plus some TV and movie executives, even celebrities. He must notice that I'm getting quieter and quieter because he spins me away from the mirror for a sec and puts his arms on the chair to lean in and say, "Vibrant Violet! You are my cash cow this season!" in a perfect imitation of Angela's voice. Then he cackles a bit and I laugh with him, glad for the release.

"Girl, you are going to knock that bitch Veronica right off the runway with that smile," Henry says.

"She really is a bitch, right?" I ask, glad for someone to talk to.

"Capital B," whispers Henry, as he starts to tease my hair. I smile and relax into the chair as he creates an insane upsweep that sits about six inches off my head. I have to admit it does make my face look lean and stark—in a very good way. With the white powder for my cheeks and chest and the dark red lipstick he paints on ("No blotting, please!"), I don't even recognize myself in the mirror. I flash back to the first day of school this year, looking in Julie's visor mirror and wondering if I'd ever see something besides a mousy, pasty, blah girl. Now I have my answer—I look like Marie Antoinette on Bastille Day—and it's blowing my mind.

I glance around, and I get the feeling that people are talking about me. Henry is raving loudly, and girls' heads are starting to turn. Not just the dressers and assistants, but the other models too. And I'm not sure it's the good kind of attention. I can feel the bad vibes in the room, and a couple of girls turn away quickly to whisper to each other. It reminds me of the day I went to Roger's fairly formal synagogue wearing shorts and flip-flops. Of course, I was eight years old and my parents should have told me better, but all the other little girls were in dresses and I felt really out of place—especially when I walked into the bathroom and caught some of them whispering. "We weren't talking about you!" the alpha girl said, which obviously proved that they *were*. That left me with a pit in my stomach, and I haven't been to synagogue with Roger since, though he hasn't been since his bar mitzvah either.

People are definitely talking about me here—I have a sixth sense about that. And Veronica Trask is shooting total eye daggers in my direction. She starts to walk toward me and I can feel my face tighten into a smile that mirrors hers. I'm learning to fake this.

"Shrinking Violet," she says. Sooo creative. Like I've never heard that before. This girl has nothing on junior high hallway bullies. She sidles up to me for a whisper, which I'm starting to see is her way of breaking people down without appearing publicly hostile. "Just because you've got Mario driving you around and Henry doting on you and Angela treating you like a princess doesn't mean you're not a flavor-of-the-week, soon-to-be has-been. Angela goes through a new IT girl every season, and I'm the only one with staying power."

Then she backs away with a smile and blows a kiss to Henry, who rolls his eyes.

"Girl, you better pipe up," says Henry. "Don't let that vampy bitch talk to you like that."

I just smile at Henry and shrug. He gives me a quick *tsk-tsk*.

I hate myself for being a doormat. And even though I know Veronica's an awful person and it's her, not me, as Julie's life coach would say, I still have this thing inside—a weakness, I guess—that makes me really care whether people like me. It's like a huge deal. I feel like I'm three years old and someone just kicked me out of the sandbox. I've always been one to wear my heart on my sleeve, though, so maybe this near-tears feeling will help with the almost-dead look I assume I'm supposed to rock on the runway.

It's almost time for the show to start, and I can't believe there's no one here coaching me or telling me what the hell to do out there. I mean, aren't I supposed to have some sort of runway trainer or Mr. Jay–like pep-talker?

I see the first few models stumbling off stage and rushing to get into their second outfits, and suddenly I'm second-to-next to go. This feels like summers at my neighborhood pool—waiting in line to jump off the high dive. Scared and thrilled and hoping people won't laugh. Knowing that once you line up, there's no bailing out or everyone will call you a chicken. But back then, I always wore a T-shirt over my bathing suit so people wouldn't see how bony I was. (Actually, I still do that most of the time unless it's just me and Julie in her backyard.) I look in one of the long mirrors now, as I'm about to step into the lights, and I see a girl I don't recognize—a girl who looks like she belongs here, among the beautiful people.

As I step out, I focus on the photographers at the end of the runway. A few flashbulbs go off, and I keep my game face on as I move down the catwalk. Even though I'm walking at the same pace as the other girls—which is a pretty fast clip—the world seems like it's moving in slow motion. No more bored-janitor-with-a-broom—I can almost feel the influence in this audience. I might have a celebrity spidey-sense. I move my head left and right, not able to fully see the people lining the edges of my stage but knowing they're all looking at me. But not in the way the kids at the pool used to look at me. They're seeing the clothes, of course, but I'm totally pulling this off. They think I'm one of them—they think I'm a real fashion model.

As I hit the end of the catwalk, where I know to turn on my toe and clear the way for the model behind me, stopping very briefly so the photographers can get a shot of my dress, I am overcome with a rush of emotion. And before I can help myself, my mouth involuntarily breaks into a huge, beaming smile. I'm hit by the heat of what seems like a thousand flashbulbs and I hear a collective gasp in the audience—it's like a movie moment and I can't believe I'm really living it. Suddenly I wish my mom and dad and Julie and Roger and—I'll admit it—the BK girls were here to see me doing this. THEY LOVE ME! After thirty seconds that feels like an hour, I strut back to the tent feeling giddy.

It's not until I get backstage that I realize I've completely fucked up. The other models are rolling their eyes at me, and one girl who I thought wasn't even an English speaker spits "Amateur" when I slip past her. *Shit!* What is the one thing Angela kept telling me? *Don't smile.* It's a rookie mistake. Now everyone thinks I'm a bumpkin from Carolina who probably won a contest and got to walk the runway. I've blown it.

And then I see Mickey running at me with Angela at his heels. Oh man, here it comes. I brace myself for a tirade and half expect them to throw me out of the show—if not out of New York City entirely.

"My starlet!" says Mickey, gazing up at me as he reaches my side. "Matt and I want you to close the show with us tonight!"

"But I've got to get into my second outfit," I stammer. "I have to go out again in a sec." I see models edging up to take the stage—I've got like two minutes before I'm up.

Angela looks around and sees Veronica. "Veronica! Come here. Take Violet's place for your second walk. Mickey and Matt will be walking her out to close the show."

I look down, not wanting to see the fury that must be dancing on Veronica's face right now. But all I hear is a peppy, "Great! I'm ready." I lift my head up and my eyes lock with Veronica's—and instead of anger I see a challenge there. It's a look that dares me to step into her space.

No time to worry about that, though, I have to get changed. Mickey seems unconcerned that the careful order of outfits that he established for the show will be disrupted when Veronica goes out midshow in a gown and then I close it in black capri shorts. Yesterday that seemed essentially important to the "integrity of the line," but right now he seems intent that I walk out with him at the end.

I change quickly and meet Mickey and Matt at the edge of the runway. Before we head out, I whisper to Mickey, "Why me?"

He looks up and says, "You lit up the photographer's pit like the top of the Chrysler Building at noontime in July. Now get that smile ready!"

We walk out to cheers and camera clicks, and some people are even throwing flowers. I couldn't squelch this grin if I tried.

After the show, I change back into my regular clothes and try to tame my massive hair hill. Waiters come backstage with glasses of champagne and little plates of fruit. "Model food," says the redheaded Australian girl I met the other day. I smile and take her comment as an opening.

"I'm Violet," I say, wiping off my powder-white makeup with a towel as she slips on some amazing brown suede boots.

"Samantha," she says. "Nice to meet you, Violet."

I notice that she has a ton of freckles—way more than me—and her blue eyes seem extra far apart. Samantha also has a space between her two front teeth. She's not the prom-queen type, but she's got a certain model look to her, which I'm starting to realize is incredibly popular with the designers, if not always all-American pretty.

We walk out of the dressing area together, and Samantha tells me to call her Sam. She's from Sydney, and this is her second New York Fashion Week. "It gets easier," she says. "But I guess you've already made a name for yourself."

"Oh, no," I say. "I think Mickey is just kissing up to Angela—that's why he had me close the show." I hate how I'm always putting down my accomplishments, but it feels like the right thing to do when someone might get mad at you for succeeding.

"Violet, don't be silly," says Sam. "You kicked ass out there. And it was worth it just to see Veronica's face when you took her spot. Though I'll have to deal with the fallout later."

"What do you mean?" I ask, pleased that Sam isn't cutting me down.

"Oh, we live together in a Tryst apartment," says Sam. "I'm sure she'll be cursing your name all week. But don't worry—I'll stick up for you."

"Wait—you guys are roommates?"

"Yeah, but it's more like we have a business living situation," says Sam, explaining that Tryst subsidizes their apartment downtown as long as they're booking jobs in the city. Apparently they even sleep in bunk beds because there's only one bedroom and four girls live in the apartment.

"You mean like in *Zoolander*?" I ask, and I can't help but let out a laugh. "I totally thought the bunk beds were a parody thing."

"Well, our apartment is sort of like a comedy show," admits Sam. "I think Angela likes to keep us in one place so she can keep tabs on us. I could rent my own apartment at this point, but I travel almost every week because I book a lot of jobs in Miami, so it's not really worth the expense. I'm trying to save money so I can quit modeling and go to college in the U.S. in a couple of years without having to work to pay my way through. Still, living with Veronica is no picnic. As you might guess, it's pretty intense."

We break into laughter together as we wander toward the back exit of the tent. "You going out?" asks Sam. And I don't know what to say. I mean, I'm not really sure what "going out" means. At home, I think it means a party that I wouldn't be invited to anyway, so I'd never be "going out." Maybe here it means that too. I don't have anywhere to go . . . but I do wonder if it might be fun to hang out with Sam a little more. She makes me laugh.

"Nah," I say. "I'm staying with my crazy aunt in Brooklyn, and she monitors my hours."

"Bummer," says Sam. "Well, next time then. This is New York City, Violet. You can't hide under the covers forever."

I wish I were the girl who'd go out, but I'm not. And I hate that Sam knows that just from spending like five minutes with me. I wanted to be someone else here, but despite the attention I got tonight, I still feel like I'd be out of place if I "went out." How lame am I? I head back with Mario in the car. Rita's already in bed when I get to her house. Big surprise there. Luckily, Julie answers her cell phone and I get to tell her all about the insanity—alien models, the runway flashbulbs, and of course my very own wicked stepsister, whom Julie dubs "Veronica the Vicious." I have to put my face in my pillow a few times to stifle loud laughter—Julie is cracking me up.

"Tell Roger I'll call him next week," I say, as we're about to hang up.

"I will," says Julie, laughing. "I just hope he can hold back his judgmental voice long enough to let you tell him some stories. I can hardly believe what you're seeing, Vi."

"I know. Ridic."

And just like that, I'm Violet of Violet-and-Julie, and it doesn't matter what that Veronica thinks.

For the rest of Fashion Week, every designer I work with asks me to smile as I hit the end of the runway. I tell each of them that they don't even have to ask—it's automatic. Angela seems pleased with the attention I'm getting—there have been pictures of me in some publications that cover Fashion Week. I'm kind of hoping I'll get to be in a magazine that my friends at home might see, but Angela says that takes months because they work way ahead of time. I guess that's why I'm modeling spring clothes in the fall.

On Friday night—the last night of Fashion Week and the day before I head home to Chapel Hill—Sam makes one last attempt to get me to go out. Maybe it's because I finally took a glass of champagne after this show (I deserve it, right?) or maybe it's because I spent the whole week being a fashion model and not one person— well, besides Veronica the Vicious—questioned whether I belonged. But I say yes to Sam, who smiles and says she knew she'd get me eventually.

"You, Violet Greenfield, are a boldfaced name in the making," she says, as she links arms with me. "So, where do you want to go?"

Before I have a chance to answer Sam's question, I hear a voice shout my name. Both of us turn to face a scuffle at the tent opening. Our big security guards are holding back three photographers. "Violet! Flash us a smile! Over here, Violet! Look here!" I can hardly believe they're talking to me, but Sam and I are the last models clearing out, and there's no one else around.

"Told you you'd done well," says Sam. "Let's try the side exit."

Just then, a preppy-looking guy in a blazer eases through the security guards, slapping hands and giving half hugs as he passes.

"Jerk alert," says Sam, turning toward an alternate exit and trying to pull my arm. But I'm staring at the blond-haired boy in the blazer. And his eyes are locked on mine as he strides toward us.

"Hello, Sam," he says, as he nears us. "Who's your friend?"

"As if you don't know, Heller." Sam rolls her eyes and looks at me. "Violet, let's go."

But I can't take my eyes off Blazer Boy, if only because he hasn't once moved his eyes from mine—even when he spoke to Sam.

"Hello," he says softly. And his lips move so slowly I think I might faint.

"Hi," I say.

Then he smiles and introduces himself as Peter Heller. "I'm a student at NYU," he says. "And a friend of Sam's."

"You wish," she says, but when I finally look away from Peter, I see that Sam is smiling, too.

"Where to, ladies?" Peter asks.

"Oh, fine, Heller," says Sam. "I'll bite. You tell us."

His eyes focus on mine again as he says, "My Place."

thirteen

My Place is a nightclub in Manhattan, and I
knew that even as it came out of Peter's rosebud mouth because
I saw Carrie and her friends go there once on *Sex and the City*. If I
hadn't known there is a club called My Place I might have fainted
when Peter mentioned it, but I still got a chill at the way Peter
looked at me as he said it. My only physical encounter with a boy
was when Tray Cleaver, a sweet kid from junior high who moved
after seventh grade, gave me a peck after school one day. I think I
probably wrote ten pages about that in my diary, and no offense to
Tray, but just Peter's *look* was more than that kiss. I felt a surge of
emotion when he said, "My Place." Like I would like to kiss him. A
lot. And for way longer than I kissed Tray Cleaver.

Peter tells me that he sent Mario home (Is it weird or flattering that
he knows Mario's been driving me around? I'll go with flattering—and
maybe just a bit presumptuous. He's too cute to be weird) and that
his car will take us down to My Place. We hop into a giant Lincoln

Navigator, with leather seats and rims that seem to have some auto-mated quality (they move on their own—again, could be weird, but not when they belong to someone this amazingly hot). He introduces his driver as Chip. Does everyone in New York roll like this?

Peter opens up a bottle of champagne in the car, and that's when I get nervous. I'm not even eighteen, let alone twenty-one. I only took a couple of sips in the tent because I felt like I should. It's not that I'm opposed to drinking, or even underage drinking—it's be-cause I'm a fraidy cat. I'm already feeling a little tipsy—I can tell that my cheeks are red because they feel so warm. But maybe if I get more tipsy I'll expose myself as the gawky outcast. So far, everyone's been buying that I'm a real model—even Peter, it seems.

"You deserve a glass, Violet," says Peter, as I put my hand up and try to refuse it. "You're the toast of the town tonight."

"Gag me," says Sam, laughing and filling up her plastic flute as she puts her feet up and trails them out the side window. "Violet, you don't have to drink anything if you don't want to."

"Oh," I say, wondering if I should try to be cool or just own up to my own dorkiness. I already noticed that I'm the only one who buckled a seat belt when we got in. I go with changing the subject. "You know, I'm not even eighteen—I don't know how I'm going to get into this club." Of course, I had to change the subject to one that makes me seem even more like a lame outsider. *Jesus, Violet!*

But Peter just smiles and reaches out to touch my cheek. *Heart. Stopping.* "Don't worry, beautiful," he says. "It's covered." Then he downs the glass he poured for me as we drive up to the club.

There's a huge line outside My Place, but Peter takes my hand and walks me right up to the front. That champagne in the tents must have gotten to me, because I can almost hear a little voice in-side me shrieking, *He's holding my hand! He's holding my hand!* But, of course, the rational part of me knows he's just trying not to lose me in the crowds of tight jeans and backless tanks that are gathered on the line. Sam has already pushed in ahead of us and gotten inside—I guess the bouncers know her. As Peter and I walk up to the front, he takes me to the inside track of the sidewalk, where there is—no lie— a red carpet. And we are walking next to—again, totally serious—a velvet rope. I kind of thought those things were exaggerations, but no.

I'm so lost in my own thoughts—the "holding my hand" voice, taking in the trappings of glamour around me, still trying to make sure I don't fall, and so glad that I wore my magic-feather boots today (Julie once told me how shoes are really important when you try to get into clubs)—that I hardly notice when people in the line start shouting Peter's name. Namely, people with cameras. "Heller, who's on your arm?" I hear one guy yell.

"Violet Greenfield," he says, beaming at me. "She rocked Fashion Week."

"Violet—are you with Heller?" the photographer shouts.

It's like I'm watching a movie. This really feels like it's on a screen and not happening in actual life. All I do is smile silently. And then Peter and I are in the club. "Sorry about all that," says Peter. "Don't pay any attention." And I don't, really, because I'm still wondering how I got in the door without showing ID. I'm half convinced that I'm sleeping in the Raggedy Ann bed right now, and Rita's about to wake me up out of this dream for some hearty granola.

Inside the club, it's dark but candlelit—there's a rainbow glow to the room, and I can feel the bass through my boots. There are beds— honest—spread out among the numerous bar areas, and people are draped across mattresses with fancy-looking cocktails. Sam is on an outdoor deck, her feet up on a gigantic bed with flowy white curtains around its four posters. There's a tabletop right in the middle of the mattress. Sam's waving at us, but the area is roped off so I'm not sure we're allowed to sit with her. Then Peter says, "There's our table."

In the distance, I can see the Empire State Building lit up in red, white, and blue. I stare at the skyline for a minute before I focus on my surroundings. I recognize a couple of Tryst girls already there with Sam, but luckily Veronica isn't anywhere in sight. As I sit down, Sam reads my mind and says, "Bad V is on the other side of the club, so don't worry." I turn and see Veronica holding court with—am I seeing straight?—Nicky Hilton. Again, I must be in the Raggedy Ann bed with a high fever. I slide onto the bed and curl my legs behind me.

"Those boots you wore for Tracetown were killer," says the model on my left.

"I know!" I say, not sure if she means "killer" like cool or "killer" like they were really hard to walk in. Both are true.

"I'm Jakele," she says, lighting a cigarette. She offers me one, but I say no. Should I have said yes?

I doubt myself probably a hundred times as I talk to Jakele and the other girls with weird names at my table, but I think I'm actually pulling off this hanging-out-at-a-club thing.

Everyone is drinking so much that I feel obliged to take a few sips of the pink concoction Peter sets in front of me. It tastes so good that I finish it off and a full one magically appears. I'm talking to Sam and laughing—I love her, I decide—and Peter keeps looking my way even when he's chatting with other girls. It sort of makes me jealous, but it's not like he's with me or anything. Wait till I tell Julie I went to a club with a college guy.

Soon we're taking a back exit onto the street where there's a line of cabs waiting. I'm a little nervous because I've been spoiled with Mario driving me everywhere and I've never actually taken a cab, but I don't want to sound dumb, so I slide into a backseat and wave good-bye to Sam. Peter motions for me to roll down the window and then kisses my hand. I could die.

I give the driver Rita's address and he seems to know where he's going, so I drift off in the backseat. In fact, he has to shake me awake when I get to Rita's house, which is both scary and embarrassing. As soon as I fall into the Raggedy Ann bed, I'm asleep.

*   *   *

The next morning, Rita shakes me awake at seven A.M.

"Up and at 'em!" she says, pulling my quilt down as she starts to strip the bed before I'm even out of it. "Your flight's at eleven, which means you'll have to get a taxi in about two hours."

"So can't I sleep more?" I ask, my voice muffled by the pillow and my head throbbing. The sunlight seems extraordinarily bright this morning, even down here in the basement.

"No, little miss out-until-three-A.M., you cannot," Rita says. Then she walks out the door and pounds up the stairs, turning once to yell, "Now GET. UP."

Eek, this sounds like I'm in trouble. Leave it to Rita to notice the one night I do anything interesting. I lie in bed for a minute, thinking about last night. It really was like a scene from my own *E! True Holly-wood Story*. I could replay the part with Peter kissing my hand over and over in my head and never get bored. That is, if I could lose this headache. I schlep to the bathroom and pop a couple of aspirins before I set my iPod into its speakers and choose the "Love" playlist. Even when I put it on random, I always end up with a good song for the game I like to play—where I name a guy, and the song that comes on is how he feels about me. As I step into the shower, Journey's "Don't Stop Be-lievin' " starts, and I feel absurdly happy (it's kind of scary how much I believe in this game that Julie and I made up when we were ten).

I let my shower linger through three songs so I'll be fully awake for Rita's wrath. Although I guess I could possibly have a hangover, I don't really think I was drunk last night. I mean, maybe a little. But I'm feeling better already so how bad could I have been? I guess the three A.M. thing is what's really bugging her.

Upstairs, she's put out fruit and granola for me and is sitting at the table. No paper, just Rita meeting my eyes. "So have you talked to your mom and dad this week?" she asks.

"Yeah," I say, though I know I have a few missed calls from them that I haven't returned. As the week went on, it just felt like I was away at camp or something (I practically *was* in the wilderness, since Rita's not online), and Mom and Dad don't like calls after ten P.M.

"Well, your mom feels a little out of touch," Rita says. "And I'm sure she won't want to hear about last night."

"Why?" I say, annoyed that Rita is putting on this all-of-a-sudden concerned-aunt act. "I just hung out with some of the girls after the show ended. We got food—that's all."

"Oh, Violet, don't start down that path," Rita says, putting on her glasses and reaching for the paper. But it's not the big paper she normally reads. This one is smaller, tabloid sized. And she's not browsing it like she normally does, she's heading for a specific page. Then she holds it out to me.

PRINCE OF NEW YORK NIGHTLIFE HAS NEW PRINCESS reads the bold headline. Underneath is a half-page photo of Peter. And me. Even though I know this is going to get me in trouble, I can't help noticing that I actually look pretty good in the photo—tousled hair, cool skinny jeans, and a purple-gray tunic with a loose leather belt that Mickey let me have after the show. My eyes do look a little bleary, though. I wonder if Rita noticed that. The caption says, "Nightclub kid Peter Heller escorts Fashion Week darling Violet Greenfield into My Place last night." Hmph. Could have been more clever.

"Princess of New York nightlife?" asks Rita. I can't tell if she's mocking me or using that disappointed-adult voice. Her tone seems to be a mixture of both. But I do realize that I'm in trouble.

"I don't know how they . . . what . . . did you?" I've never been in trouble before—never done anything exciting enough to cause worry—so I'm stammering through this.

"Don't worry, sweets," she says. "I didn't tell your parents. Yet. And I know you weren't out every night—I clocked you in at around eleven P.M. the rest of the week, so I figured you weren't into this scene and I'd give you your space."

"You were awake?"

"Eh, awake enough, Violet," she says. "Your Aunt Rita's not as blind as you think."

Then my cell phone rings. I pray it's not Mom. I look. It's Angela. Almost as bad, but I guess I have to face her sometime.

"Ultra Violet!" she sings, as I pick up the phone. "Love you in the *Post* today! Peter Heller's girl? It's perfect. Isn't he a dream? Use the photo op, but don't get involved. And I love that you don't have a drink in your hand, darling. Good girl. Remember, you're a role model now—that's how you land the cover of *CosmoGirl!* Chin up, drink down—you're a natural."

Like so many times when I'm talking to Angela, I really don't understand what she's saying. But she seems proud of me, and she doesn't give me room to voice anything but a "Thanks, Angela." Then she says, "I'll see you soon, my number one V!" And she's gone.

"Your agent?" Rita asks.

I nod, still bewildered by the newspaper in front of me.

"I'll bet she's happier than a pig in shit right now," says Rita, and I realize how surprised—and grateful—I am that she hasn't called Mom yet.

"So . . . am I in trouble?" I ask.

"Well, honey, not with me," she says. "And don't worry—I won't show this to your mom."

"So are you mad at me?" I can hear my voice tremble a little. I hate that I feel like I'm five years old, but I can't help it.

"Violet, I'm not," says Rita. "Hell, I'm surprised you didn't party every night this week—and I'm proud of you for that. But I don't want you to get into this crowd. It's what I've been worried about from the beginning."

"You've been worried?" I ask.

"Well, sure," she says. "You're my little niece, and the fashion world has big teeth. I don't want you to lose yourself, Violet."

Okay, here's where I start to tune out. She keeps talking about how I am special and blah, blah, blah. It's the same speech my parents give me when I get down on how plain I am. But this time, the speech is coming from a different place—because I'm kind of being told my being plain *is* what's special about me. I'm not buying that.

Aunt Rita finally stops talking and clears her dishes. Despite the rant, she's actually being pretty cool, and she leaves me to eat my breakfast in peace and let this whole *New York Post* thing sink in— luckily there was no article with the photo, so it's probably not that big a deal. I have to admit that even though I know I shouldn't have gone out last night, and that photo is probably going to get me grounded or something, it's sort of thrilling to see my face staring back at me from the dining room table. And it's not the plain face I am used to seeing in my bedroom mirror. It's New York Violet. It's Violet on the Runway. She's daring and wild, and people think she's beautiful. I'm not sure this new me is someone I want to give up.

fourteen

For the whole plane ride home, I'm trying to figure out how to spin the *Post* thing for Mom. After-show party that was completely mandatory plus hack reporters who need a sensationalized caption? (Rita says everyone knows the *Post* isn't too into fact checking.)

When Dad meets me at baggage claim, I get a big bear hug and it seems like he almost has tears in his eyes. "You look beautiful, honey!" he says. "Where did my little girl go?" Mom's driving the car around in circles waiting for us to emerge from the airport, and she has the same emotional reaction. They're acting like I've been gone for weeks. Weird.

On the ride home I tell them about the shows and how I smiled but people seemed to like it. I even brought up the *Post* photo, but left out the part about the champagne and the Navigator with rims. I also didn't give them the exact wording of the caption. I don't think you can buy that paper in Chapel Hill, so I'm pretty sure I'm safe.

Mom says something about asking Rita to mail us a copy, but she's forgetful and she probably won't follow up. I'm lucky she has no Internet skills. All in all, the debriefing goes well. As soon as we get home, I drop my bags and run to the computer to IM Julie and Roger (a.k.a. "Diane Sawyer" and "RC1"—for Rivers Cuomo, not RC Cola, as Roger has to explain every now and again, much to his annoyance). They're both logged on and waiting for me.

RC1: Welcome home, Iman.

Roger prides himself on using correct capitalization and grammar, even on IM. "It's the little things," he says.

DIANE SAWYER: DISH!
VIOLET GREENFIELD: cannot go into this on im. elmo's at 7?

I'm not really looking forward to school on Monday, but I've been waiting all week to meet Julie and Roger at Elmo's—our favorite diner—and tell them about my adventures. We agree to meet there for dinner.

Mom drops me off in the parking lot of Carr Mill Mall. It's an old cotton-factory-turned-strip-mall, but part of it is charming, with wooden walls and a faint, pleasant, musty smell. I'm the first at Elmo's, and I take a booth by the window, grabbing crayons and one of the cartoon papers they give to little kids to color. I can't wait to see Julie and Roger, so I take out my nervous energy on the paper and end up with a blue and purple chicken drawing as Roger walks in.

"My, my, can it be? A *superstar* at Elmo's?" he shouts, as he strolls toward my table. People mostly ignore him, but I still turn red.

"Roger!" I give him a big hug, and it seems like he turns a little red too. He sits down across from me.

"So? Did Naomi throw a shoe at you? Did Kate offer you a line in the bathroom of the Viper Room? Are you pregnant with a rock star's love child yet?"

I laugh and show him my chicken scribble.

"Very cryptic answer, Fräulein Greenfield," he says, scratching his chin.

Then Julie bursts in. "Violet!" She plops down next to me on the bench.

The next hour flies by, even while an angry waiter stares at us as we let our sweet tea refills get watery without ordering dessert. I tell them all about everything—even Peter Heller. I try not to look smitten when I mention him, but Julie says, "Uh-oh—Brian Radcliff has some competition!"

"He sounds like a sleaze," says Roger, chewing a straw to bits in his mouth. I roll my eyes at him, and he sticks out his tongue. It's good to be home.

"So what'd I miss at school?" I ask, not wanting to be a spotlight hog—even though I've been talking about myself for like an hour nonstop.

"Not much," says Julie, eyeing Roger intensely. "Just a math test really."

"Wait—did something happen?" I ask. "You guys are sharing a 'Don't tell her' look."

Roger looks down at his mostly devoured burger. "Um, well, you know, you were on the Style network."

"I was?!" I scream. "No way! When? What time? Did you guys see?"

"Roger!" says Julie in a loud whisper (uh, as if I can't hear them . . . *Hello*—I'm right here). "We said we weren't going to mention the . . ."

"The what? The TV thing? Consider it already mentioned! Now tell me what the problem is," I say. "Did I look hideous or something?" Suddenly I'm convinced that's why they're acting weird. I *did* look hideous, and they were trying not to break it to me.

But Julie rushes in because she knows my thoughts have already run wild in the "I'm a tall ugly freak" direction. "No, Violet—you looked gorgeous!" she says. "Seriously amazing. Like envy-inspiring, drop-dead, *America's Next Top Model* beautiful."

The weird thing is, when Julie normally goes into these pep talks, I totally blow her off and don't believe her. Like the time I got upset about my brother saying my hair looked permanently dirty because it wasn't really blond—she told me my hair was "flaxen colored," which meant I could be the star of a romance novel one day. I kept crying anyway because I can never bring myself to trust people's compliments. But when Julie says I looked good on the runway, I believe her. Because while I was in New York, I felt it. I felt the energy around me and people reacting to me with awe. They saw something in me—like the way Julie and Roger see something in me.

"So what's the deal?" I say. "If I looked okay, then why the weirdness?"

Roger looks up at me, and I can tell he's just been biting his lip, which means he's nervous. "Shelly Ryan brought in a tape of that Tracetown show to school," he says. "She's telling everyone that you're really tight with her and she's the one who got you the contract with Tryst."

"She's basically using you to make herself even more popular," Julie snorts, disgusted. "All the underclassmen girls are eating it up and begging to be in her fashion show."

I sit there for a minute, unsure of what to say. I know I'm supposed to be completely annoyed and angry at Shelly. Roger and Julie expect me to go to school on Monday and tell everyone she's lying.

But part of me doesn't want to do that. *Shelly Ryan is bragging that she's tight with ME?* I can't help but be a little bit excited.

At school on Monday, it's like the first day of school I wanted to have. I get up the courage to wear *the* boots, and I ditch my glasses for contacts. I even have on my skinny jeans, but the cashmere sweater is a little much, so I'm just wearing a white ribbed tank top. (Julie is all about being PC and gave me a speech in the car about not calling it a "wifebeater," but Roger and I still do behind her back.)

In the hallway on the way to my locker, I can hear ripples of people talking about me as I walk by. Not in the way they normally do when they mock my height, but in an awestruck and envious way. It feels like . . . I'm popular. As if to physically prove this, the BK are standing by my locker when I get there. Shelly squeals when she sees me. "Violet! You're back!" She gives me a gigantic hug, looking around to see who's watching this scene. I glance over my shoulder too, and it seems like the whole hallway has frozen in order to observe our interaction. Roger and Julie are a few feet behind me. All the way here in the car, Roger was rubbing his hands together maniacally and talking about how I was going to take down Shelly and her lies this morning when I got back. How I'd tell everyone that we weren't friends and that she was just mooching off my opportunities.

But that was his plan. Mine was different.

"Hey, Shelly!" I say, smiling. "Hi, Tina! Hi, Jasmine!" I glance at Roger and Julie over my shoulder.

"Violet, can you meet us after school to plan the fashion show?" says Shelly, not so much asking as assuming. "Of course you'll be the star—with me—and we need to practice walking together! Like sisters!"

I can feel Roger's cringe. He's still waiting for me to lower the boom on Shelly's fakeness. And I know she's awful and not my real friend. And I know Jasmine and Tina are incredibly empty vessels without opinions or senses of humor or—let's be honest—original thoughts. And I also know that if I hadn't been at Fashion Week, Shelly Ryan wouldn't be talking to me except to insult me. But still. It's like this is what I've wanted *my whole life*. To be part of the group of girls who own the school. Who wrap teachers around their fingers and never sit at home alone on a Saturday night. Who walk around laughing and smiling and being watched and adored by everyone else.

"Sure—I'll meet you out on the quad," I say.

"Perf!" says Shelly. Then the BK swish their little hips down the hall, and I'm left with Roger and Julie, who roll their four eyes (six if you count Roger's glasses) in unison and leave me in silence. I've still got an audience of underclassmen, who are trying to look at me without me noticing—weird how you can feel that kind of thing— but I don't even pay attention to them. I think I've just betrayed my two best friends in the world for a shot at prom queen. And I'm not sure whether I'm sorry.

In class, all the teachers are super nice to me, and a couple even ask me about modeling and tell me about a time when they lived in New York City—which is sort of awkward since it's not like I really know the places they mention. On the plus side, it doesn't seem like I've missed much work at all, and I'm glad to use my lunch period to make up a math test—I can avoid facing Julie and Roger. I don't even have to see them after school, since I'm meeting up with the BK, and I notice as I head out to the quad to see Shelly that Julie and Roger are already pulling out of the parking lot without even asking if I need a ride. Ouch.

But Shelly, Tina, and Jasmine are standing by the big tree, ges-turing frantically at me like they've practiced synchronized waving.

"Hey, guys," I say.

"Um, we're not *guys*," Tina laughs. "We're girls. Hello. We're girly girls!"

I might vomit in my own mouth.

"Yeah," says Jasmine. "That's like one of Shelly's biggest pet peeves—when girls say 'Hey guys' to each other. Ew."

"God, bitches, shut up," says Shelly, overpowering both of them not only with her tone but also with her body language. They shrink behind her as she links her arm through mine. "It's totally fine to call girls 'guys'—it's just an expression. Duh!"

I guess Shelly really is taking this New Best Friend thing seriously. We stroll over to a bench on the quad, and she and I sit down. Jasmine and Tina—no lie—sit on the grass at our feet. "Now, let's start thinking about the show," says Shelly, as Jasmine takes out a pad and paper, presumably to take down every single word that comes out of Shelly's edict-proclaiming mouth.

Just then, I see the boys from the basketball team walking out of the math building with their gear. I spot Jake near the middle of the pack. I haven't talked to him much since I've been home—he's always on the phone or out of the house now, and when he's home his door is shut. I try to catch his eye, and I wave, but he doesn't see me. Some of the guys do, though, and they start to migrate our way. I guess that's what happens when you're Shelly Ryan—guys flock.

"Hey, Shelly," says a guy I recognize as Nathan Heath, a popular junior. Then he floors me by saying, "Hey, Violet."

"Oh, um, hi," I manage to stammer.

"Saw you on TV," he says. "So you're a model, huh?"

"Well, I . . ." I start, but then Shelly nudges in.

"Violet and I are going to be together on the runway at the University Mall fashion show. Tickets go on sale Friday, Nathan. You should totally come. You all should." Shelly gestures to the group, which pretty much feels like the whole team at this point. We must have fifteen guys clustered around us. I notice my brother hanging back and looking down at his shoe as he kicks a large rock. I'm no body-language expert, but I think he's uncomfortable.

"Hey," I hear. I look over and see Brian Radcliff smiling at me and making me completely forget about my brother.

"Hi," I say, smiling back. I don't feel nervous. In fact, in this moment I feel downright desirable.

"We'll all be at the show if Violet the professional is there, right guys?" he says, looking around at the team. A resounding round of "Hell yeahs" and "Damn rights" echoes, and I see my brother walking away, toward the gym, on his own. The guys wave good-bye, then turn and head to practice as Brian Radcliff gives Shelly a kiss on the cheek and says, "See you later, baby."

Shelly, Jasmine, Tina, and I plan to meet on Friday to sell tickets to the fashion show together at a table at lunch. Then Shelly agrees to drive me home and insists that I sit in the front seat. I expect Tina and Jasmine to give me icy stares like I got from Veronica when I stole her spot in the Tracetown show, but their irises seem blank as always, and they happily climb into the backseat like obedient little lapdogs.

At home, we have a family dinner where Jake talks to Dad about basketball and Mom talks to me about a few calls that she got that day from local newspapers wanting to interview me for some town flavor features. I promise to call the reporters back, though I can't imagine what I'll talk to them about, and Mom says I should call Angela first in case there are things I shouldn't mention. *Yeah, like the pink drinks at My Place.*

Staring at my beloved popcorn ceiling that night, I think about the two worlds I'm in and wonder how to meld them. Do I like Brian Radcliff? Or Peter? Am I Violet the runway model, or Violet the BK geek-to-chic project? I'm so not sure. But what I do know is that I'm no longer Shrinking Violet the no-name wallflower. And as I drift off to sleep, I think, "Good riddance to her."

fifteen

Julie and Roger are barely speaking to me.
Or maybe I'm barely speaking to them. In the car on the way to
school, they gave me a ton of shit for hanging out with the BK. It
went something like this:

> **Julie:** "Shelly Ryan is like *the* Mean Girl, Violet. She's been
> stomping you down since second grade."
>
> **Roger:** "Think about it, Vi. Who's mean at age seven? Only
> the truly evil Damien-like children of the world. You
> could be in mortal danger here."
>
> **Julie:** "And don't think we don't know why you're doing this.
> Being friends with those girls is not going to make up for
> the name-calling pain you've gone through for being tall.
> It can't fix that."
>
> **Roger:** "Yeah. In fact, it makes you pathetic."

And that's when Roger crossed his arms and Julie sighed and things deteriorated. The ride ended in silence, so I guess we're back where we started. At first I felt kind of bad about befriending the BK, but it doesn't seem like Julie and Roger are even willing to discuss it with me. Julie's always had other friends in different social groups—the drama kids, the newspaper kids, the debate kids. I never bug her about that. But the second I get some new friends she's all whiny. And Roger. Well, he never likes anyone besides me and Julie so I guess he's just being consistent.

But I'm so busy that I don't even have time to think about my friends hating me. I try to say hi and tell them about things, but they act so uninterested and cold that I stop trying. Shelly wants to hang out almost every day and hear stories from New York. She asks me about each moment and what the clothes I got to wear looked like and who were the prettiest other models. She even says she'd like to meet Angela. It's like she cares more than my so-called "real" friends do.

Same with the theater crowd—working there has become a total ego boost. My manager, Richard, is all about being my captive audience in the lobby area between shows. It's a Wednesday night, and he just gave me permission to take next week off so I can help Shelly finalize plans for the mall fashion show. Tonight he even sets up a little runway of flattened cardboard boxes. He wants me to show him my walk and re-create the smiling thing.

"I read all about it in *WWD*!" he says. I only know what *WWD* stands for—*Women's Wear Daily*, a fashion industry trade magazine— because an editor from there called to interview me. The article said I had "fresh appeal at the tents."

I kind of like telling the New York stories to my co-workers— they really listen to me and look at me like I'm incredibly cool. I think before they just thought I was the boring high school girl who liked to drink Sprite through a Twizzler straw (Roger taught me that when we were in third grade).

"Did you meet Anna?" asks Richard, breathless and on the edge of his red polyester lobby seat.

"Um . . . ?" I really don't know what he means, but it seems urgently important. To him.

"Wintour! Anna Wintour!" he screams. "Of *Vogue*? Oh, Violet, you're hopeless! You need me up there as a culture coach. Like Jai on *Queer Eye*! Let me come!" He claps his hands together and stands up to walk his cardboard runway. The rest of us break into laughter and applaud his walk. Sometimes I think I'd do this job for free.

When I get home from my shift, Mom and Dad are sitting in the living room, reading, which is how I know something's up. They always read in bed.

"Hi, honey," says Mom. "You got a phone call from *Teen Girl* magazine tonight."

Whoa. Turns out it was actually a call from Angela to tell me that *Teen Girl* magazine wants to use me in a fashion shoot they're doing.

"She says you don't even have to do a . . . a. . . . oh, what do they call it when you try out for these things?" says Mom.

"A go-see," I say.

"Right, no go-see," says Mom. "They just definitely want you."

To me, this is bigger than the runways. Because everyone at school will see *Teen Girl*, and there'll be lasting, tangible proof that I am not a nobody. Still, my parents seem kind of upset.

"That's exciting, right?" I say, not really sure why Dad's worry lines look deeper than usual.

"Yes, Vi, it really is," he says. And then there's a pause as he looks at Mom. "We're just concerned that . . ."

"That things are happening really quickly, and you may not be ready for all the changes," interrupts Mom.

"What changes?" I ask. "I'm still me. Just more confident because I've found something I'm good at. That's all."

"Well, this would mean going back to New York for a few days next week," says Mom. "And Angela's been talking about all the people who want to interview you and photograph you."

"Wait," I say. "Are you guys censoring things for me? You've only told me about a couple of interviews. Am I missing something?"

"We didn't want you to get overwhelmed," says Mom. "But yes, Angela's been calling me at work, and I've been keeping what I have you do to a minimum."

In fact, I've been interviewed by about four places in the past few days—including the *New York Times*, which was pretty exciting. Shelly asks me about each one and then makes me feel really important. Julie, on the other hand, said, "Oh," when I told her about the *Times*. Roger scowled, but I saw a gleam of respect in his eye—he's been reading the paper daily since last year so he can advance his "smarter than everyone" theory.

"How much of a minimum?" I ask, suddenly wondering if this *Teen Girl* thing is one of many cool offers that my parents are hiding from me. *Momager alert!*

Dad hears my tone. "Violet, this is for your own good," he says. "You're still in high school—you can't be off posing for sexy billboards and fashion magazines!"

"Wait—are you saying I got offered a billboard? Other magazine shoots? And you're keeping this from me?!" I'm getting mad now, but seriously, why is everyone trying to stop me from being a model? It's the one thing that makes me feel good about myself! And that's what parents always say they want—that "oh, just so you're happy, dear" bullshit! "You guys are as unsupportive as Roger and Julie!" I yell. "I can't stand this!"

"Honey, what's going on with Julie and Roger?" asks Dad. "I haven't seen them around the past few weeks."

"Don't try to change the subject," I say. "I want to know about what calls I'm getting. They're MY calls. They're not for you, not for Mom, not even for Angela. People are asking for ME!" I do realize that I'm sounding like a total brat or one of those girls on *My Super Sweet 16*, but I'm feeling indignant. I hate it when I'm kept in the dark—especially about things that affect *my* life.

Dad sighs and looks at Mom. "Okay, honey," she says. "We're all tired. How about I make a list of the people who've called and their requests? We can go over it tomorrow night at dinner, okay? Then you and me and your dad can figure out what will work."

She's being very rational, but I'm still fuming a bit. I feel like the whole world is trying to thwart my big moment! "Fine," I say. "Good night." Then I stomp up the stairs and into my bedroom. I would slam my door but the stomping was pretty loud, and I think I've made my anger clear. No need for overkill—that might seem immature.

I log on to IM just to see who's there. I see that "ShellBelle" is on, but I don't really feel like talking to Shelly after I blew up at my parents. "Diane Sawyer" and "RC1" are both idle, but I bet if I sent them a note they'd hear the *doodle-do* of the computer and pay attention. Maybe Roger's lying in bed reading the autobiography of Lenny Bruce. I should probably stop him—he's already read it like six times.

I type, "yo rivers," but I let my cursor hover above the Send button too long and I end up erasing the message. How have I become afraid to contact my best friends? Maybe it's because we've barely said two words to each other lately. Shelly drives me to school now, and I have to admit that even with the New York experience to fill up our conversations, we're running out of material. I miss witty banter and substantial topics. *Sigh.*

I turn out the light and lie in bed for a while, thinking. Is this what popularity is like? A lot of attention from random strangers, but not much from the people you used to call your friends? Julie and Roger must be jealous of my new social status. I talk to Brian Radcliff almost every day now, and I've been at three parties with the basketball guys, who all pay attention to me and know my name. Julie was jealous when I got to go to Fashion Week—she even admitted it—so she must be mad that I'm eclipsing her at school. Well, that's just too bad. I don't know if I can be friends with people who get so jealous when like one cool thing happens in my life. That's not fair—is it?

sixteen

The next night at dinner, Mom drops a bombshell: Angela wants me to move to New York and live in the model apartment. I'm guessing it's the one Veronica and Sam live in. Mom and Dad actually seem open to the idea. Or at least not totally against it, especially since Tryst will be paying my rent. Jake leaves the table early, and I can hear him on his cell upstairs.

"Violet? Hello?" Mom snaps her fingers in front of my face, which—by the way—is never really okay.

"Sorry . . . what?" I guess I got distracted when Jake got up. He's been super quiet around me lately. I think he's uncomfortable that his basketball friends are my friends now too, but he doesn't have to be so completely weird about it. You'd think we'd be closer since we travel in the same social circle.

"I'm asking you what you think about New York," says Mom. Looking in her eyes, it actually seems like she wants me to go. I glance over at Dad. Total poker face.

"Um . . ." I don't know what to say. I've just started to ensure that I'll close out my high school career on a high. I'm popular! And I get to go to parties. At this rate, I'll definitely have a prom date. But what am I thinking? Have I already forgotten about the rush of the runway lights? Seeing myself transformed in shoddy-chic tent mirrors? Holding Peter's hand by the velvet rope?

"Yes! I do want to go!" I say. Dad coughs, and I realize I'm going to have to sell this idea.

"Technically, I have enough credits to graduate after I finish this semester," I say. You only need four English credits, and I got an extra semester's credit for all the tutoring I did last year. In all other subjects, three credits is enough for a diploma.

Dad raises an eyebrow.

"And colleges will totally love something like this for the end of high school," I say. "It's practically as good as volunteering in another country—but more original. Plus, I'll earn some money to put toward tuition."

Dad smirks a little. "You could earn some money that would help cover costs," he says, looking at Mom.

"Angela says your day rate could be five hundred dollars to start," she says, frowning slightly. "That's a lot of money for a girl your age. And I'm sure she'll appreciate her fifteen percent cut."

"I could send you guys the money I make," I say, hoping to persuade them to let me go. "You can keep it in savings and just give me what I need—I promise I won't be irresponsible."

Mom raises her eyebrows at Dad. "Well, the contract is only a trial for five months—and Angela has said Tryst will pay for seventy-five percent of your housing costs if you live in their apartment—the other twenty-five percent will come out of any paychecks you get from modeling work. But you have to follow their rules, and the first time you don't show up for a meeting will be the last."

Mom says that final sentence in an imitation of Angela's voice, and then she chuckles. I grin, realizing that Mom is convincing her-self that I should go. "You could have Rita keep an eye on me," I add. "She totally looked out for me last time!"

"Was that the last time when you called me exactly one time in a whole week?" says Mom, but she's smiling. I can tell they've already talked about this and decided to let me go if I want to.

"Well, honey, you'd be leaving for college next fall anyway," says Dad, breaking into a full grin. "If you really want to do this, I guess you should take your shot."

I leap up from the table and run to hug Dad. Mom stands up and yes, it's a three-way.

"There are more ground rules, young lady," says Dad. "But we can talk about them later. I'm sure you want to run up and call Julie."

I smile and excuse myself. It's like I have to pretend that I am going to call Julie so that Mom and Dad won't realize we've grown apart. Instead, I go up to my room and call Shelly. She screams and says she has to four-way in Jasmine and Tina so they can hear the news too. They greet it with bubbly "Yays" and "Awesomes," but as I hang up the phone I still have a nagging urge to call Julie.

Just then, Roger IMs me for the first time since last Sunday, when all he did was tell me *Goonies* was on TV—and when I tried to write back to him he logged off. This time, he says:

RC1: Is ShellBelle there?

VIOLET GREENFIELD: haha. no, dummy.

RC1: Mean-a Tina? Jackass Jasmine?

VIOLET GREENFIELD: of course not. those drones?

RC1: What a way to talk about your new BFFs.

VIOLET GREENFIELD: they are not my bffs!

RC1: Coulda fooled me.

VIOLET GREENFIELD: well my real bffs are being pretty lame

RC1: Oh, really? How so?

VIOLET GREENFIELD: let's see . . . cold shouldering me at school

VIOLET GREENFIELD: being nonresponsive when i have amazing news

VIOLET GREENFIELD: generally acting kind of

And here I pause. Because saying someone might be jealous of me isn't something I'm used to doing. It feels weird.

RC1: Kind of what?

VIOLET GREENFIELD: jealous

There. I sent it.

RC1: Surely you jest.

VIOLET GREENFIELD: well what then?

My phone rings. Julie.

VIOLET GREENFIELD: brb

"Hey, Julie," I start. "I'm so glad you called because I have the most amazing . . ."

"Violet!" she stops me. "I can't believe you're accusing me and Roger of being jealous. After I already had the whole jealousy talk with you and owned up to it. Like we'd be jealous of the robots you're hanging out with now."

I look back at my IM screen. "RC1 has signed off." Coward.

"Why are you and Roger talking behind my back?" I ask. "This is like that bad phone scene in *Mean Girls* when the other girls are listening in on the conversation. Wait—is Roger on the line?"

"Don't be paranoid, Violet," says Julie. "We were IMing too, and he told me what you said. I just need things to be clear between us."

"Fine, so clear it," I say.

"Okay, well I am not jealous of the BK, if that's what you're thinking," she says. "And look, if you're really having fun with them, talking about whatever the hell they prattle on about, then fine. But Shelly is really using you, Violet. She's not a nice girl."

Back to this again. "Well, she's nice to me," I say, and even as it comes out of my mouth, I know it isn't true. I mean, she's sort of nice. But she doesn't really care about me any further than I can add to her legend at school. I know that. But still, it's fun to be noticed and to be flirted with and to have Saturday night plans beyond *SNL*.

"Fine," says Julie. "Then I guess you've got a new best friend."

I feel like someone punched me in the stomach. I want to tell Julie that she'll always be my best friend, but I also feel this selfish pull to live in the popular world—just this once. I'll go back to being plain old Violet later, but I can't let it go just yet. And that's why I stay silent.

"Well it looks like there's nothing else to say," says Julie. "Later."

I hear her click off, and it feels scarily final.

part two

violet
VIRTUOSO

seventeen

       I turned eighteen in December, and I also got an early diploma from Chapel Hill High School. Shelly tried to get me to throw a big party, but I wasn't into it. I had to give up any trips to New York in the meantime to focus on finishing all my credits, so I lost the *Teen Girl* job, but it's worth it because now I get to move to NYC full time. I did get to do one photo shoot down here with a photographer from "the City"—that's what New Yorkers call their hometown, I've learned—and now I have a real model book and a card with a few studio shots and some outdoor settings. It was so much fun—the photographer just kept telling me what a natural I was, and Jake said my head was big from that for a week. Angela put some of my press clips in the back so people will remember that I was "that Violet Virtuoso" from Fashion Week. I've been really focused on talking to Angela and planning my "career"—how crazy is that? I can't believe I'm actually doing this, but I'm on the plane so it must be real.

Mom and Dad and Jake were hard to say good-bye to—they all drove me to the airport like it was the last time they'd see me or something, even though Mom and Dad were coming up to New York in a month to visit. But it is a big deal, I guess. It's kind of like moving away from home.

When I get to LaGaurdia Airport in New York, I find the taxi line. Mario isn't going to be driving me around now, Angela tells me. I guess there's probably a new girl she's wooing who gets that VIP treatment, but that's okay—it was strange for me anyway and I think it made the other models hate me. My goal this time is to make friends—I'll need them if I'm going to be here for a few months.

Sam gave me good directions to the apartment—which is *waaay* downtown. She told me that's called the Financial District, and when the cab drops me off I see a lot of hurried men in suits who look important. Or at least like they think they're important. As I look around for number seventeen, I see a familiar figure leaning against a gray stone building. "Peter?" I can't help but break into a wide grin as he suavely takes off his D&G sunglasses (I can see the sparkling label from twenty feet) and saunters toward me. Even in a bulky winter coat he looks hot.

"Need help with your bags, ma'am?" he asks, reaching out to give me a hug. It's funny how he's only nineteen but acts like some adult. It's almost like he's my older-man crush. We crash into each other awkwardly (I haven't quite learned the hug-hello etiquette that seems pervasive in New York) and then he takes my bags.

"Sam told me you were coming in today," he says. "I've been waiting here all afternoon for my princess."

I smile at him. Do people really talk like this? I have to admit he's making me blush. It's official—I'm back in the crazy fashion world. And this time I've got my own apartment.

Well, sort of my own. When we walk into 4B, there are clothes strewn everywhere. A bowl of half-eaten raisin bran that's beyond soggy sits on the glass coffee table, which is covered with magazines.

"Hello?" I say, sounding more like a scared five-year-old than the independent woman of eighteen I keep trying to pretend to be. Peter is right behind me, and he walks in with my bags like he owns the place.

"I doubt anyone's home," he says. "Sam's on a shoot and—"

We hear a rustling in the bedroom and the door opens. Veronica Trask, in a flimsy, see-through gray tank top and cherry-patterned underwear, emerges. Her eyes are half-closed and smeared with steel gray shadow. "Welcome to the dollhouse," she says, barely looking at me. "Hi, Peter."

"Veronica," he nods, moving past her down the narrow hallway with my bags. I wonder if seeing her toothpick body in underwear is as awkward for him as it is for me, but I'm not about to make a big deal out of it. I'm still not sure how things work around here, so my intention is to watch and learn.

"Wait—" I say, as Peter starts to open the door Veronica just came out of. "Isn't that Veronica's room?"

"It's a one-bedroom, Suburbia," says Veronica, as she heads into the bathroom. "And the bottom bunks are taken."

It's hard for me to believe that a superstar like Veronica Trask lives in a one-bedroom with other girls, but Angela prepped me for tight quarters. She says since everyone travels so much for photo shoots and fashion shows, the apartments are more like a place to keep things than a living space.

In the dark bedroom, there are two bunk beds on opposite walls. One blocks half of the only closet in the room, which is overflowing with bags and boots and clothes. Peter sets my bag on an empty top bunk with no sheets that's incredibly far from the tiny window. I can't help but think of the tenements we learned about in AP History last year. But we do have a doorman, so I guess it's not exactly on par with early-twentieth-century immigrant city life.

"There are sheets for your bed in the closet," Peter says.

"Are you always the welcome wagon for new girls?" I ask.

"Nah—you're special," he says, touching my cheek with the back of his hand. Suddenly, I just know he's going to lean in and kiss me right here. In this dreary room with bunk beds and messy sheets and mistreated designer shoes. I start to close my eyes and then his lips are touching mine, so softly and gently that I'm surprised I don't melt into a pool of hardly-ever-been-kissed butter right there. Just when I'm about to get really lost, though, he pulls back.

"Well, Violet," he says. "Looks like you're all moved in. I'll check in with you later—I expect you to hit Marquee with me soon, of course."

"Of course," I whisper, like I'm Jasmine or Tina following Shelly's orders. I'm proud that I let him go then and don't continue the babble that goes on in my head. Things like, "I'll come with you anywhere, whenever you want," and "Will you call tonight? Please?" I am incredibly pathetic, but I will certainly not act that way. Not here.

So instead, I change the subject. "I wonder what's taking Veronica so long in there," I say.

"Don't worry, Vi, she's blowing rails in there," says Peter. "Which means she'll come out in a better mood."

Not a clue what that means, but I don't want to admit that I'm ignorant, so I just nod and smile and make a mental note to Google the phrase later. Maybe she has an eating disorder? I did see some people who seemed like they might at the tents, but I've never really been up close and personal with one. Well, unless you count the way Julie and I obsessively followed Mary-Kate Olsen's progress.

"Do watch out for Veronica, though," says Peter. "She's been talking some heavy trash about you these last few months."

"Really?" I say, suddenly feeling a little sick.

"Yeah, but it's just because she's threatened," he says. "She's only living in this model apartment because her career has gone down the tubes since she passed out at a Paris show two years ago—she did a stint in rehab, and everyone's still a little scared of booking her. But I guess Angela believes in her because she lets her live here."

"Oh, that's sad," I say, feeling like I understand Veronica's mood swings a little more.

"Don't pity her," Peter says, grabbing his coat and heading for the door. "She'll hate you if she senses that. Stick close to Sam— she's a good egg."

I wave at Peter as he winks at me and slips out the front door. I'm not sure what to do with myself after he's gone. Veronica's still in the bathroom—not that if she came out we'd have a big bonding conversation, but it's oddly quiet. I call Rita to tell her I made it, and she says she's out in the garden but would love to chat later and take me to lunch. So much for familial support. Angela asked me to check in, so I try her office and leave her a voice mail.

Then I sit down on the futon couch (after brushing off some powdery crumbs—from donuts?) and pick up an issue of *Cosmo*. "101 Ways to Make Him Beg for More" offers a little distraction, but I'm not quite to the stage where I'd try oral sex with a jar of applesauce yet. Then I flip to the fashion pages and there is Veronica, looking sultry and chic on location at a horse farm. She's wearing equestrian-inspired designs and posing—rather seductively, actually— atop gorgeous horses.

And then, suddenly, there she is in front of me.

"I did that shoot last fall," she says. "God, I'm so fucking sick of working with animals."

"Oh, you look beautiful," I say, wanting to play up to her good side and also genuinely impressed with the fact that Veronica went into the bathroom looking like a beat-up raccoon and emerged in a strapless-dress-over-white-tee-with-cinched-leather-belt ensemble looking fresh-faced and runway ready.

"Yeah, well, we have a casting in twenty minutes," she says, smiling.

"We *what*?" I look down at my sweater and jeans.

"Get it together, Violet," says Veronica wickedly. "We don't want to be late."

I'm too frazzled to recognize the full evilness of this moment, and I run into the bedroom and grab the old skinny-jeans-and-cashmere-sweater ensemble from my bag, kissing the Prada boots, which have provided so much stability for my fragile style. I also say a little prayer thanking God for the messy-bun look as I pull my hair up in the bathroom mirror and quickly finger-brush my teeth. I paint on some black eyeliner—Henry always did that at the tents to make me look more "sophisticatedly sloppy"—and choose bright red lipstick. Better to look Parisian chic than like a little girl from the country, I figure.

"Ready!" I say, and Veronica opens the door for me.

"Nice work, Violet," she says. "The quick change is a highly valued skill in this world." Then we're out the door and in a cab. I can't help but wonder who we're going to see—Veronica looks so sweet and pure.

"So what's the casting?" I ask.

"Oh, didn't I say?" she purrs. "It's for *Teen Girl*. They like a natural, fresh-from-the-heartland look."

I curse her silently as I frantically rub at my black-lined eyes and fuck-me red lips, which only makes me look more like a hungover hooker. This is going to be a long five months.

At the casting—which is held at *Teen Girl*'s headquarters in midtown, a huge all-glass building with a giant fountain wall in the entrance—I manage to find a bathroom and properly remove my overdone makeup. But still. Now I've got no kind of glow—just the postflight pasty look. Veronica, on the other hand, has the bookings editor laughing and smiling as she snaps Polaroids.

And then it's my turn.

"You're Violet, right?" asks the bookings editor, as I walk over to the white wall where she's snapping photos of all us wannabes.

"Yes, Violet Greenfield," I say, trying to smile as I count insecurities in my head: *Does my breath smell? Is my hair greasy? Am I blinking spastically because my contacts are glued to my eyes after the flight?*

"I remember you from the shows last fall," she says, holding the camera up to her face so I can't see her expression. Did she like me in the fall shows? Or did she think I sucked? "You were great!" she says, bringing down the camera after she's snapped three pics—one smiling, one pouting, one "with attitude" (I just try to look angry and it seems to work). "We wanted to book you after that—where did you go?"

"Oh, I was back home in North Carolina," I say. "I had to finish high school."

She starts laughing. "How sweet," she says. "Well, welcome back, Violet Greenfield." And then she's on to the next model.

In the cab on the way back to the apartment, I go over my conversation with the booker. She seemed to like me, but did she think I was silly? That I dropped out of sight for too long? And then it's like Veronica reads my mind.

"Too bad you had to go home after the shows," she says. "You had some buzz going around the end of October."

"Really?" I ask cautiously.

"Oh, yeah," says Veronica. "Everyone was wondering about Peter Heller's new arm candy—the girl with the huge grin who walked the runway in such a funny way that she didn't even seem like a real model."

Okay, *ouch*. But is Veronica actually telling me I was hot for a while here? She takes out a compact mirror and reapplies her ballerina-pink lipstick as I stare at her and wait for her to continue.

"Too bad the buzz is gone," she says. "Stay away too long and you're a has-been before you ever were." With that, she snaps her compact closed and asks the cabdriver to pull over.

"But where are we?" I ask.

"Spring Street, Violet," she says. "I have another casting here." She hands the driver a ten-dollar bill.

"Oh, okay, should I . . . ?"

"No, sweets," she says. "They didn't ask for you at this one—it's mine." She says those last two words with a quiet but intense authority, as if she's talking about more than just this one casting. Then she's gone.

I take the cab the rest of the way back to the apartment and flop down on the dirty futon. Sam isn't home yet, and the only noise that interrupts my thoughts is the buzzing of the refrigerator every now and then. I dig out my iPod and put on James Blunt. I wonder if I missed my big chance. I mean, last fall, *Teen Girl* was calling and not even asking me to do a go-see, but today I was up against like thirty other girls.

I scroll through my cell phone, wishing I could call Roger—he'd make me lighten up, or he'd at least have some genius way to mock Veronica, which would help. He and Julie did say good-bye to me on the last day of school before winter break, but it was like, "Hey, good luck in New York" from Roger, and a sarcastic "You'll do great—after all, you're a BK girl" from Julie. I still say she's jealous, but we haven't really had an actual talk since the night she denied it on the phone. Somehow talking to Shelly doesn't appeal right now. I toss my phone onto the coffee table and stare at the blank walls. There aren't even any posters up in here—it's like some depressing hospital waiting room, but without the fake flowers.

Then the house phone rings. I hesitate for a minute before I pick it up—should I? I do live here, so I decide to be brave.

"Um, hello?"

"Hello, Miss *Teen Girl!*" It's Angela. She must think I'm Veronica.

"Hey, Angela," I say. "It's Violet, actually."

"I know my V from my V!" says Angela. "You booked the *Teen Girl* shoot, Violet."

"I did?" I say, still not sure she knows her Vs. "Seriously? What about Veronica? She was like perfect for them."

"Oh, they worship her, of course," says Angela. "Everyone does. But she's twenty now and, well, everyone also likes a new face—and you're it. We'll get you in all the teen books to build your name, and then we'll move on to *Elle* and *Vogue*—"

"Oh my God," I say, suddenly imagining my face on *Vogue's* cover.

"Then we'll see about getting you an ad campaign," she continues. Again, no idea what that means, but Angela sounds excited so I say, "Great!" and let her keep talking.

"So the *Teen Girl* shoot will be tomorrow at ten A.M., Violet dear," she says. "And it's at 494 Broadway . . ."

I rush around the living room looking for a pen and paper, repeating the address in my head so I won't forget it. *So much for my buzz being dead, Veronica,* I think to myself. *It's just starting to build.*

When Sam gets home later she gives me a big hug, and I fill her in on the casting. It's so incredibly nice to feel like I have a friend here.

"Rock!" she says, when I tell her I booked the casting even after Veronica tried to sabotage me. "You showed that bulimic Barbie!"

"Is she really bulimic?" I ask, half-scared, half-intrigued. "Peter said something about her 'blowing rails' in the bathroom this morning, but I wasn't sure . . ."

"Oh, jeez, he probably shouldn't have said that," says Sam.

"Oh, I know," I say. "Bulimia is really serious, and I wouldn't ever bring it up or anything—don't worry."

"No, Violet," says Sam. "He meant she was doing lines of cocaine in there."

Whoa. Hello!

"I mean, we're all a bit bulimic, right?" Sam chuckles, and stands up to go into the kitchen. "Edamame?" she asks.

"Sure," I say, glad I at least know what *that* means. Julie used to obsess over getting enough fiber, so she ordered those peapods constantly.

"Um, Sam?" I say, still trying to process the drugs-and-eating-disorders info I just got. "Just so you know—I don't really do cocaine."

"Yes, Violet," she says, in a patronizing tone, as she sits back down and sucks a couple of beans out of the green pod. "That I suspected. For the record, neither do I. Veronica's the only one here who really has a habit, and she keeps it out of our way, so no biggie."

"Hmm, okay," I say, still furrowing my brow and trying to navigate my next topic. "And also, I'm not really bulimic. I mean, I've never made myself throw up or starved myself or anything."

"Well it's not like I do it that often either, Violet," says Sam. "And don't worry—once you get your first 'she still has that baby fat' comment from a photographer or editor, you'll figure out how to pull the trigger pretty quickly."

I half-smile and nod, wondering how to react. It's like a Movie of the Week around this apartment.

Over the course of the night, I notice that Sam just polishes off the edamame beans, even though I offer her some pasta, which is all I can find in the cabinets. Luckily there's parmesan cheese too, and a little fake butter, so I can make the one dish I know how to cook. I want to tell Sam about the kiss that shook my knees this afternoon, but she warned me about Peter in the fall, so I'm not sure what her reaction will be. I decide to keep it quiet for now, like something just for me, which feels sweet.

We discuss our schedule this week—we're supposed to call Tryst each morning to see if we have a casting to go to that day—and Sam shows me her Treo. A Tryst assistant can remotely program it with castings or bookings the minute they're scheduled—Roger would *so* love that, but I've had a little notebook calendar for years, and I'm kind of attached to the old-school way of keeping my schedule. Besides, Sam says if I do use a Treo, Tryst will take a little extra out of each check I earn as a "phone fee"—I'm so not into hidden charges. Sam tells me about the best cafés in the neighborhood, as well as where the nearest gym is. We have a membership at New York Sports Club through Tryst, so I guess I'll have to start working out. Because whatever Sam may think, I'm so not getting an eating disorder. What a cliché.

eighteen

I get to the shoot twenty minutes early the next day. I just really don't want to be late. But no one's at the studio, so I sit outside on the curb and read through the latest issue of *Teen Girl*, paying close attention to the fashion spreads and how the models pose.

At ten-thirty A.M., just as I'm triple-checking the address I wrote down in my archaic calendar notebook and getting really worried that I'm in the wrong place, a frazzled-looking brunette carrying two large bags and a drink holder filled with four coffees pulls out a huge set of keys and starts jiggling the door to the studio. She doesn't see me until I stand up, and then she looks really surprised.

"Are you the model?" she asks.

"Um, yeah," I say. "I'm Violet, and I thought I was supposed to be here at ten?"

"Right. Well, I'm the photo assistant at the magazine, and my boss is on her way—she'll be here at like eleven."

"Oh, okay," I say, as we walk into the studio. "I just thought . . ."

I must sound pathetic because then she puts down her coffee and smiles at me. "Sorry, Violet, things always start really late. In fact, the models are usually the ones who hold us up, so they'll be impressed that you got here before noon. My name's Eva, by the way."

I smile at her and look around the studio. We're standing in a little kitchenette where Eva is sorting the coffees. There are long curtains hanging around a stagelike area in the loft space. Across the curtained area, I see a room with lit mirrors—I guess for hair and makeup. "This is beautiful," I whisper.

"First time in this studio?" Eva asks.

"Um, first time at a photo shoot," I reply.

Then Eva spits out her coffee. "What? Really?" She laughs.

"Yeah," I say. "I'm pretty new. I just did Fashion Week in the fall, but I haven't done a photo shoot yet. I mean, except for my book stuff."

"Hmm," says Eva, leaning on the kitchenette's marble counter. "You might want to keep the 'first photo shoot' thing to yourself. I don't think we work with newbies very often."

That makes me incredibly nervous, but I try to be cool. I walk around the studio and stare out the big windows, down to Broadway where people are carrying shopping bags and deli coffees, starting their busy city mornings. It sort of makes me want to hum "Nine to Five," but I'm pretty sure that's not cool. The editors and photographers finally arrive around eleven-thirty, and I'm in the lit-mirror room practicing faces. I keep wishing we were doing a horse farm shoot like Veronica's—or maybe something with a few girls. It's weird that we're in a studio and it's *just me* in the shoot.

There's a makeup woman there who doesn't talk much, but she does put an inordinate amount of foundation on my face. Also, she pokes my eye when she curls my lashes, but I'm too nervous to protest and she's not paying attention to me anyway. She's busy talk-

ing to the photo editor—I guess they're friends because they're talking intimately about what they did last night. When she's finally
done with my face, I feel so drag-queeny that I ask the editor if this
is the way I should look.

"The lights wash you out," she says. "You do know that, right?"
and then she rolls her eyes and says to the makeup person, "Models." They laugh. And I'm like, *Hi. I'm right here.* But no one seems
to think I can hear. Or feel, for that matter.

The shoot is for the April issue, and it involves me and about ten
umbrellas in different colors. It's bizarre to be wearing spring
clothes in winter, but at least we're not outdoors. For the first shot,
I'm in a shorts-overall set with bright red buttons, wearing a bikini
top underneath. It's completely something I would never wear—nor
would any of my friends—but when I ask the stylist if teens some-
where do wear things like this, she seems annoyed and says, "Ever
heard the word *aspirational*?"

Note to self: Just be quiet.

The photographer keeps telling me I'm "singing in the rain" and
that I should smile like I'm "a ray of sunlight coming through a
cloudburst." The only thing that's really making me laugh, though,
is Eva. She keeps miming funny faces behind her boss's back. Whenever she does that, I break into a smile and the photographer yells,
"Perfect!"

The thing is, though, this isn't very much fun. I mean, on the
shoot for my book, I was completely pampered and everyone was
telling me how beautiful I was. Here, I'm less pampered and more
prodded. The makeup woman keeps coming up to me with a hard
bristle brush to reapply something. A few times she even spits on her
finger and then wipes at my eyes—is that sanitary? The fashion editor keeps ducking into the shot to move my arms or reposition my
legs when I don't respond fast enough to her orders of "Elbow

down! Move that knee!" The photographer, between saying "Perfect!" talks more to the photo editor than to me. Which would be
okay except that they're talking *about* me.

"Do you think her head is a little elongated?" he says.

"We can touch that up in proofs," she says.

"What about the freckle problem?" he asks. "The makeup can't
cover all that."

"Don't worry," she says. "We'll take them out later."

"And her chin at that angle—ew. Violet, pick your head up a bit!"

It goes on and on like that. When I do the shoot in a way-short
tennis dress, they put a fan on me. As my hair blows around they comment on how its texture is so fine that I seem bald. Nice. After a quick
lunch break (catered trays of vegetables and chicken—everyone seems
surprised when I load up my plate) they bring in a hair person to
give me extensions for the fan shots.

Despite all the abuse, though, I stick to my "don't talk" rule.
Every time I open my mouth, I give away that this is my first shoot,
so I might as well stay quiet. Eva comes over to say hi while I'm
chowing on my second helping of chickpeas in the corner.

"You're doing great," she says. "No one would ever know it's
your first time."

"Thanks," I say, wondering if she's someone I can confide in. I
think of how she was imitating her boss earlier and decide that she
can't be too bad.

"Can I ask you something?" I say.

"Sure."

"Do they always talk about models like that?"

"Like what? You mean, *Oooh, look at her chicken neck?* Or *What's
up with that snaggle-toe?*"

I laugh and a chickpea shoots out of my mouth. Then Eva's
laughing too.

"In short," she says. "Yes. They're awful. I've worked on dozens of photo shoots and I can safely say they treat everyone like they'd treat a lamp or a chair—*no feelings, no thoughts, can't hear us.*"

"That's terrible," I say.

"Yeah, I guess it is," she says. "To be honest, though, I never really even thought about it. Models aren't usually the friendliest, and most of them act like they are so above you, so it kind of seems okay when the photographer talks about them like they're objects. Like it's bitchy-attitude karma."

"Well, it's painful for me," I say, feeling vulnerable.

"Violet, I think you need to thicken up that pale skin," she says. Then her boss calls for her, and she runs off to fetch a third coffee, knocking me on the arm as she goes.

I know she's right.

The rest of the shoot goes the same way—more comments as if I'm a deaf, dumb, blind, mute thing that just happens to hold up the clothes they want to show off—and when I get home I find out that I've got a few more go-sees this week. Luckily, Sam wrote down the messages so I know I'm not being led astray concerning what to wear to meet certain magazines. One of the calls is for *Nylon*, which I've never heard of. When I tell Sam that, she sits me down and shows me this very high-end magazine with thick, glossy pages and giant fashion spreads. Kind of like *W*, but not so huge.

"It's a really good booking to get," says Sam. "It moves you into high-fashion territory, even though they only pay like a hundred-dollar day rate." It's so funny to me to hear people like Sam and Veronica talk about money. They act like a hundred dollars a day to stand in front of a camera is below minimum wage or something.

Sam also tells me that being treated like a lamp, as Eva so eloquently put it, is pretty standard. "Just don't interact with them," she says. "And let anything they say roll off your back. It's not like they're hot enough to be in front of the camera, so you have the edge. They're just jealous."

By the next Friday, I've been on twelve go-sees and done two more shoots, including one for *Nylon*, which scared me. I had to wear a see-through shirt without a bra. I did it, though, and I only cringed and whined internally, because I've seen reality shows where models refuse to do things and it always seems so lame. I'm definitely learning to keep my mouth shut and pose, and it's paying off. I felt sexy at that shoot, and it wasn't just because my nipple may or may not have been showing. Sam was right—if you just remember that you're the one in the spotlight, it's much easier to drown out the whispers of the photographer and editors. I even try a mantra she told me to repeat in my head as I'm posing: *I am beautiful. I am powerful. I am a golden goddess.* Somehow, even though it's cheesy, it makes me feel really hot. I will never, however, tell Roger that I have a mantra.

Even though Tryst takes out more from my checks than I thought they would—a twenty percent agency fee, plus a little bit of each check to pay for part of the apartment and as reimbursement for things like my original model-card shoot—I'm earning like ten times what I'd make at the movie theater. But everyone keeps telling me that landing an advertising gig—as opposed to an editorial shoot—is where the money is. Sam says she's been trying to get a big campaign for months so she can save enough money to move out of the model apartment. I can't imagine living alone, even though I must admit the bunk beds are a little ridiculous. Besides, I'm trying to save my money for college.

I'm mailing my checks to Mom—she has a checking account for me at home so I can just withdraw from ATMs up here when I need cash, which I hardly ever do. I mean, Tryst is subsidizing my apartment so it's really not that expensive, and I've been getting so much free stuff it's amazing. Eva even let me take home the outfit I liked the most from the *Teen Girl* shoot. The only thing I'm spending cash on is food, really. If I continue to get bookings like I did this week, I'll save up so much that I might even be able to travel internationally next summer, which has been this huge dream of mine forever.

Angela calls to say that *Teen Girl* loved me so much they want me for a group editorial shoot next week—no go-see required. Between the automatic bookings, the full go-see schedule, and that kiss from Peter (which I replay every night as I'm falling asleep), I think I might just be a rock star.

I've talked to Shelly once. She wants to come up and visit, but she's getting more and more annoying. Here's how our phone calls go:

Shelly: Violet! Who have you met with lately?

Me: *Glamour, CosmoGirl!* and *Seventeen*.

Shelly: Oh my God! *Seventeen* and *CosmoGirl!* Did you get to wear anything expensive? How did they do your eyes?

Me: For go-sees I was natural, but then I did a shoot for *Nylon* and they gave me a blue smoky eye, which was pretty eighties.

Shelly: I'm so jealous, Violet! And not to be rude but I'm just as pretty as you, don't you think? So did you talk to Angela about me?

Me: Um, I haven't really had . . .

Shelly: Violet! Do it this week! Show her the DVD I sent you of the fashion show—just the end where I do my signature twirl if she's busy.

Me: Okay, Shelly, I'll try.

Shelly: Love ya!

It's enough to make me want to bang my head against the wall. And there's no way I'm showing Angela the DVD of the mall fashion

show we had last November, which was so low-budget I almost
bailed last minute. Back then I thought, *Who am I to bail on Shelly
Ryan?* Now that I'm up here, though, I'm realizing that I'm a *model*.
That's who. By the end of the week, I've stopped returning her calls.

When Peter shows up at the door on Friday evening, I'm glad to
see him, but I don't show that too much. He can't know that I am
dying for him to kiss me again. He's been texting me all week, but
this is the first time I've seen him since move-in day.

"Violet, you look stunning," he says. I'm wearing a simple, loose,
black cotton minidress that is practically permanently fitted to my
body because I wear it every second that I'm not at a go-see. It's way
comfortable but still cute if someone knocks on the door. Not that
anyone ever knocks for me, but Veronica is friends with some of the
male models who live in an apartment upstairs, so they come by and
as they talk to me all I can think is, "You are breathtakingly hot." I
can't even keep their names straight, but I don't want to get caught
in frump clothes. Sam took me shopping at H&M on Wednesday
(maybe because I hadn't changed out of my skinny jeans in days), so
now I have a few pieces that are "model appropriate." I got excited
to tell Julie that models shop at H&M, but then I remembered that
we're not really talking.

"Thanks, Peter. You look great too," I say. And he does. White
button-down, slightly open at the top, black blazer and black pants,
hair in a soft-but-styled wave.

"So, dinner," he says. And it seems like that should be a question
but somehow it sounds like a pronouncement. Not that I'm going to
refuse.

"Oh, okay, let me just change," I say.

"You look perfect," he replies.

"Well, let me grab a belt," I say, as I run into the bedroom to dig
through the pile of clothing on the floor. Sam cinched a superwide
brown leather belt around her black dress last night and it totally

made the outfit. I also ditch the ballet flats and pull on my lucky boots—it's cold outside. I glance in the cheap full-length mirror that hangs on the back of our bedroom door. *Julie would be proud*, I think with a pang.

"Lovely!" says Peter, as I grab my coat. "Some nights it's better to be seen casually."

"Seen?" I ask. He just smiles and holds out his arm. Then Veronica comes out of the bathroom. Where, I might add, she's been for like an hour. I try to steer clear of her as much as possible because I'm completely scared of drugs. And she's mean. And she intrigues me beyond belief.

"Heller," she says. "Taking the new girl out for a test drive?"

"Don't be crass, Veronica," he says. "It's especially unattractive when you're high."

She shoots up a finger—guess which one—and slams the door to her room.

"Should we invite her out?" I ask.

"Oh, she'll be out," says Peter. "It's Friday night."

We go for Japanese food at some unmarked restaurant in the East Village where we have to walk down shady, narrow stairs. I'm worried at first, but it's gorgeous inside.

"Wow," I say, staring at the deeply red pillow seats and the hanging lanterns—not to mention the amazingly beautiful women who are mostly with well-tailored men who look twice their age. "Everyone in here looks like . . . someone."

"Everyone in here *is* someone, Violet," says Peter. "That's why it's perfect for us."

He orders a bottle of sake and a bunch of dishes I've never heard of, but everything is delicious. By dessert, I've had four little shot-sized glasses of sake and I'm feeling pretty electrified.

"So are we going to My Place?" I ask, as Peter puts his gold American Express card back into his wallet. It's almost as if I'm pretending to be someone else. Someone fearless.

"Tempting," says Peter, "but I thought we'd go to Marquee. I'm throwing a little party there tonight."

The line at Marquee stretches for an entire block, but Peter walks us right up to the door. Photographers try to snap pictures of us, but this time Peter blocks me with his jacket—he holds it over us as we pass through the VIP entrance.

"Thanks," I smile, a little breathless at the thought of how close we are.

We head over to a table where a few of the other Tryst girls, and Veronica, are already on their second five-hundred-dollar bottle of Cristal. Sam's in Florida on a shoot for *Maxim*, so I'm glad when Peter sits down next to me and starts whispering in my ear about who's who in the club. Hip-hop legend? Check. Infamous DJ? Check. Young Hollywood starlet with someone who's not her reported boyfriend? Check. I have a glass of Cristal, and it's almost like I'm hovering above this scene: me in a club at a VIP booth, sitting with models and a hot guy who happens to be my date, at least for tonight. I throw my head back and laugh at Peter's jokes, imagining all the while how alluring I look. Man, this champagne is good.

Then Peter gets up to talk to someone, and I feel a flash of the old insecurity. That's when Veronica leans in.

"Want a shot, Virginal Violet?" she purrs. I can't tell if she's being nice or condescending. Probably a little of both. She really is Shelly Ryan times ten. And before I know it, we're linking arms and pounding tequila. I don't get much down, though. It tastes so wretched to me that I actually spit it all over the table and even spray the girls across from me a little bit, one of whom I recognize as the close-cropped-hair girl who stared at me so intensely when I first went to the Tryst offices.

Veronica's laugh echoes through the club. She's thrilled with my spit-spray display, and she pounds on the table with her feet in delight, sending even more glasses crashing. As much as she's a whirlwind of disaster right now, she looks stunning. Her long, dark hair is hanging down in layers over her deep brown eyes, and she's got these insane Steven Tyler lips that are bright red tonight. She's wearing a white silk tunic that hits just above the line of her teensy black velvet shorts. A huge, gold antique-looking locket swings from her neck as she bangs furiously on the table. I find myself staring at her, wanting to be her—in a worse way than I wanted to be a BK girl when school started. This is serious. Veronica Trask is worthy of idol worship on a whole 'nother level.

She grabs my hand and pulls me to the dance floor, and I feel like I'd follow her anywhere. We spin and shake—she even gets a shout-out from the celebrity DJ, and she points to me like I should get some attention too. Things are sort of hazy, but I can tell people are watching me and Veronica dance—a crowd is gathering around us. Veronica is thriving on the energy—I can see it in her face—but I'm starting to feel kind of sick.

And then a wave hits me, and I bolt. I'm not sure which way the bathroom is, but it doesn't matter—I have to try. Suddenly, Peter is there, catching me as I stumble through the crowd. He puts his arm around me and practically carries me to the restroom. And I am grateful. Ever so grateful.

The next morning I wake up in a bottom bunk—Sam's. She must not be back from Florida yet. I'm still wearing my dress and boots from last night, but someone has kindly removed the belt. I'm facing the wall, so I swing my head around to see if anyone else is in the room. It sounds like a simple movement, but it feels excruciating. The teensy bit of light coming through the bent part of our blinds is like a searing flashlight focusing on my eyes. I close them tightly again and tune my eyes to the bottom bunk across from me. Veronica's there, I can see by the sheet-covered lump. Her head is under a pillow. She must not be a creature of the morning light either.

When I get up to go to the bathroom (a process that takes a full three minutes because I have trouble walking and my head feels like it's being clobbered by two giants with sticks), I splash water on my face before I look in the mirror. I know this can't be good.

And it's not. Between the mascara smudges and the teabag-sized puffs under my eyes, I look like the frog prince of death. I swish some mouthwash and head into the kitchen—I'm starving. It's only after I've scarfed down an entire bag of Pirate's Booty and a liter of Diet Dr. Pepper that I start to piece together the details of last night.

Peter . . . sake . . . Marquee . . . Cristal . . . Veronica . . . shots . . . dancing . . . and, oh yeah, the vomit hour. I remember getting very close to the fancy Marquee toilets. And then I remember something else. Veronica. She was holding back my hair for me. Right there in the oversized, overly plush (especially for my purposes) stall.

Does this mean we're friends?

nineteen

Sam comes home from Florida around four
P.M. and wakes me up from a blissful sleep. I'm surprised to find I
feel almost well again, but unfortunately I feel so sober now that I
start to regret last night, which I promptly summarize for Sam.

"I wonder where Peter went," I say, more to myself than to her.

"Well, he went *home*. The better question is who he went with,"
she laughs.

That actually stings more than I wish it would, but I try not to
show my feelings to Sam. Enough of Violet wearing her heart on
her sleeve.

"What was I thinking?" I say, hoping the little laugh I let out
covered my Peter pang. "My parents would die. Thank God I'm not
living at home right now."

"Well," says Sam, reaching into her bag. "I do hope your parents
don't read New York papers."

Not again.

"Page Six," says Sam. "You've got a new nickname."

I turn to page six, which is an ad for cheap flights. "I don't . . ."

"Oh, sorry," says Sam, grabbing the paper. "Page Six isn't actually on page six. It's a gossip column."

Um, okay.

So Page Six (which is actually on page twelve) has a photo of me, Peter, and Veronica coming out of what must be the back exit of Marquee. Veronica is beyond ephemeral, of course, and Peter looks great—he's flashing a megawatt grin at the photographer, which is semi-annoying. Still, even beside those two photogenic wonders, I don't look entirely out of place. Veronica and Peter are obviously supporting my weight, and though I'm definitely on the bad side of four A.M., I look kind of . . . glamorous.

"Teenage Wasteland," says Sam.

"Huh?"

"I didn't know you partied like that, Violet," she says. "You have this whole 'country girl from North Carolina' act."

"Oh, it's not an act," I say. "I really never drank until that first time in the tents with you." Well, unless you count the time Roger, Julie, and I split a six-pack of wine coolers while watching *SNL* one night when my parents were out of town. "But what did you mean by 'nickname'?"

"Did you just look at the photo without reading the words, Violet?" Sam laughs. "Acting like a real model already. Check out the caption."

"PRINCE OF NIGHTLIFE AND THE DOUBLE V: Club promoter Peter Heller escorts former top model Veronica Trask and runway newcomer Violet Greenfield out the back exit of Marquee early this morning."

Sam is standing up by the house phone. "Dude, ten new messages?! You guys were really sleeping the dead sleep."

"I didn't even hear it ring," I say, still trying to figure out if this

Page Six mention is bad or good. I mean, I know it's bad if Mom sees—so I'd better call Rita and do damage control—but maybe it's good for my career?

"Veronica turned the ringer off again," says Sam. "It's a wonder she has the presence of mind to do that on a drunken evening but she can't pick up her clothes off the floor any day of the week. You've got a call from Angela . . . make that two . . . uh, three. You'd better call her back."

I pick up my cell phone and realize it's also been off. There I find messages from Angela and Roger, which is a nice surprise. He's just saying hi, but I can't deal with him right now. I dial Angela.

"Double V, darling—brilliant!" she coos. "Was it Veronica's idea or yours?"

"Oh, I think they just . . ."

"No matter! Love it! And now that you're eighteen I don't mind much what you do as long as you make your castings—just steer clear of the powder, darling. Veronica could be in Milan right now if she didn't mix it up so much. But forget I said that. In fact, all off the record—especially if Mommy calls, okay, Verboten Violet? My star!"

Then she's gone. That went well. A text comes in from Peter. He's going to Marquee again tonight and wants me to join him.

"Dinner?" I write back. I can't believe how much of a flirt I'm being. But here, I'm starting to feel like what Angela just called me—a star.

Just then, Veronica emerges from the bedroom. I wonder if she's been in there all day. Is that even possible? Sam rolls her eyes over her shoulder at me, and I smile. But I'm not really annoyed with Veronica. In fact, I feel like we might have gotten closer last night.

Over the next few weeks, Veronica and I average four nights a week at My Place or Marquee or Bungalow 8—another exclusive celebrity hangout. Veronica says in the summer we'll hit the roof deck of the Hotel Gansevoort—they have an amazing pool. Every once in a while, Peter takes me out to dinner, but often he has work to do for school. I admire so much how he balances NYU and club promoting—he's super busy, so I don't mind when he just meets me at a club for a late night. We've actually made out six times now, and I'm starting to want to get him alone, but that's impossible in my three-person bedroom. I still haven't seen his place, but part of me is scared to ask about it. What might that imply?

Spring Fashion Week went well too. Mickey and Matt hired me as their closing model because of what they called my "smile appeal" last fall. And I booked twelve shows this time—which was really exhausting but "a fantastic image builder," as Angela put it. She thinks I might be able to book a major campaign soon for a designer, like Kate Moss did with Calvin Klein when she was about my age.

The *Post* has taken great joy in Veronica and my exploits, and the "Double V" nickname has even caught on around town. At castings, my name is linked to Veronica's—and that's pretty amazing. I've done a few more editorials, and I'm waiting on a call from Voile, this *huge* French fashion house, for a huge campaign—their new fragrance.

Around the house, things aren't as I originally expected them to be. Sam travels a lot—she seems to book tons of sunny location shoots—so I rarely see her. And Veronica has taken me under her wing. We've been shopping together and even to Pilates a few times. She goes out almost every night, I've noticed, and sometimes she doesn't come home.

I'm having so much fun that I have no time to miss Chapel Hill—Mom complains when I call only once a week, and Roger had to call me two more times before I got back to him. But they just don't get it. I'm busy. Like Angela says, I'm building something here. I haven't pulled the "I'm eighteen, I can do what I want" speech with Mom and Dad yet, but I very well might if they keep badgering me about what I'm wearing in photo shoots and whether I'm going out. I guess Rita hasn't told them anything about the *Post* documenting my nightlife. I've had a couple of lunches with her to pacify her, but she's so in her own world that we barely talk about modeling—just her pottery. I don't mind keeping it that way as long as she doesn't rat me out with Mom and Dad. As far as they know, I'm just their little girl posing for some teen magazine fashion pages.

Tonight as I try to perfect a purple-tinged smoky eye in the bathroom mirror, I'm thinking about how my *Teen Girl* shoot should be on the stands in a few weeks. I cannot wait. I hope it makes everyone at home super jealous. It's Saturday night, which is the best press night, and we're going to My Place. The paparazzi come out for Kirsten Dunst and Ashlee Simpson, but they'll settle for models, I've learned. Sometimes when Veronica and I get silly, we call ourselves *Dubleve*, which is "W" in French but sounds like *Double V*. It entertains us.

I'm borrowing a dress from Veronica tonight, and it's kind of risqué. It requires double-stick tape to keep my nearly B cups in place—the neckline redefines the word *plunge*. But it's a lavender silk and Veronica said, "Violet will thrill in violet," which convinced me. I'm also hoping that maybe Peter and I can spend more time together tonight, so I want to look extra sexy.

When we get to My Place, Veronica and I pose for photos outside the club. I've gotten used to the paparazzi calling my name, and Veronica and I oblige them for a couple of minutes. We've only been in New York papers so far, but Veronica says it won't be long until I graduate to *Us Weekly*—at least in those front sections where they show off dresses. Wouldn't that just shock the shit out of Julie? She hasn't called me, and I texted her once when I was tipsy in a cab on the way home—just "hey"—but I got no response, and I've been trying not to think about it. As I stare at the flashbulbs and strike what I've come to think of as my signature pose (though it looks suspiciously like Paris Hilton's), I'm sure I'm having way more fun than Julie is anyway.

It's an average Saturday night, which means a few bottles of champagne and Veronica running off to the bathroom every few minutes. I've definitely learned how to handle my liquor better than I did the first night when we were at Marquee; I can drink half a bottle of Cristal now without throwing up—and I hardly ever get hangovers because I drink lots of water before I go to bed.

Peter comes over to the table, where I'm sitting alone for the moment while the other girls are outside smoking. That's a vice I haven't picked up yet.

"My precious Violet," he says, slipping into the booth and putting his arm around me. Yes! I feel a makeout session coming on. "You look especially radiant tonight."

"Thanks, Peter," I say. "You too." Despite my newfound confidence, I am still a dork around boys until I've had like four glasses of champagne. I'm only on number two.

"Smoke break?" he asks.

"Yup, I'm here holding down the fort!" *Dork. City.*

"Good," Peter says. "That gives us a moment alone." We start kissing then, and his arm brushes my double-stick-taped breast, which is completely thrilling. Suddenly, he's kissing my neck and his hand is lightly touching said breast. We're in a dark corner, so I am pretty sure no one can see us, but I still hope the double-stick tape holds—I do not want to play peek-a-boob. I let him keep touching me, though, because it feels amazing. And—hello!—because he's the first guy to try for second base with me. And suddenly he's trying to get to third. His hand moves to my thigh. I'm still tingling with excitement when his tongue touches mine, but my legs are involuntarily creeping together as Peter's hand travels up past my skirt. When he gets to the edge of my panties, I gasp. "Oh, Violet," he moans. But my gasp wasn't the kind he thought he heard.

"Stop!" I shout. Peter backs away from me, wide-eyed, and I realize my volume level was up a teensy bit high. A few people near our booth had turned to look, and now they start to whisper to each other. "I'm sorry," I say, turning to Peter, who still looks taken aback. "I just . . ."

"It's okay, Violet," he says, smoothing his adorably coiffed hair. "I understand." Then he stands up and walks away from the table just as Veronica returns, energized as usual after her bathroom trip.

"Let's dance!" she says, tugging at my arm. She doesn't notice that my eyes are getting moist. I'm silent for a minute while she pulls at me, wishing Julie were here. But she's not. And I do not want to be the weeping wallflower.

"Shots?" I say suddenly.

"Yes! I knew you had a badass in you, Violet," Veronica says, as she gestures to a waitress.

A pile of shot glasses later, I haven't exactly drunk away my tears. In fact, I'm a blubbering mess. I'm lying down with my head in Veronica's lap. She's stroking my hair and giving me sympathy as I tell her about how inexperienced I am with sex and how I think I might be in love with Peter. At this moment, I really think I am.

"It's okay, sweetie," slurs Veronica. "We all have prude moments." She's smiling and a little bit of spit hits me each time she talks, but it's comforting to be sitting with her. I feel like I could fall asleep right here.

But Veronica gets me into a cab before I pass out, and I wake up the next morning to Sam lugging her suitcase into the bedroom.

"Late night?" she asks.

"Yeah," I say, pointing to the bottled water and aspirin that has made its way into the bunk with me.

"Well, it's almost noon," she says. "Brunch?"

Over a much-needed bacon, egg, and cheese sandwich at our local diner, Sam and I are pretty quiet. I've gotten closer with Veronica lately, as unlikely as that sounds, and I haven't confided much in Sam for a while. While Sam reads the *New York Times*, I page through the Sunday *Post* to see if there's any Double V coverage from last night. I have to admit it's thrilling to see myself in the paper, especially because the people at the *Post* seem as eager to make me into a star as I am to become one.

But when I turn to Page Six, I see a headline that isn't quite star making. "VIRGINAL VIOLET: Is Heller's new girl the Princess of Prudes?"

twenty

Sam tries to comfort me when she sees the *Post* story, but it's not working. Not only is the headline completely humiliating, but the story is filled with quotes from Peter and Veronica about how I'm an inexperienced Carolina girl without a sense of the modeling business or the city. Peter actually said, "New York eats girls like Violet for breakfast. Veronica and I are initiating her into the club of the city's elite. But it's not easy." Then there are quotes from Veronica about how I'm frightened by men's advances, speculating that I'm a virgin! The reporter added his own snarky commentary about new models like me being a naïve dime a dozen.

"But did you see this part?" says Sam. "The part about how your face has captured photographers and the public alike? And how you're still up for the Voile campaign?"

"Yeah, I saw it," I sigh, trying to think of the article like Angela might. She's always saying that having your name in bold print is never a bad thing. But inside I feel my chest clench, and I can't fight the tears that well up in my eyes. *How could Peter do this to me? And Veronica?* I feel like I was just starting to trust that I could live here and lead this glamorous life with good friends. That I didn't need Julie and Roger anymore.

When I get home and check my e-mail, I realize that the *Post* story has been picked up by every blog in town. Which means my friends at home will surely read it. Then my phone rings—Roger. I should have known he'd be all over Gawker and Pink Is the New Blog today—Sunday is when he catches up.

"Violet, hey," he says softly when I answer. I tried to give him a cheerful, "Hi!" but I can hear by his tone that he already knows about the *Post* story.

"Roger, I know you probably saw—" I start.

"Hey, Vi, it's okay," he says. "I mean, I did see it but I just called to see if you're okay. No explanations necessary."

"Really? No judgment?" I say. "Wait, who is this? I thought you were Roger Stern."

"Ha-ha," he says. "Seriously though. Are you okay?"

"Oh, yeah," I say, realizing that I don't want to give in to my urge to cry again. I can't let people from home know that my life is anything less than amazing. "I have a shoot for *Jane* magazine this week—for their fashion well."

"Um, okay," says Roger. "But that's not really what I meant. I mean, how are *you*? I was thinking of coming up there to see you over spring break. I know your parents are visiting, but my dad said I could fly up just for a weekend or something if you want."

My heart sinks a little. Having Roger here would be incredible, but I also can't quite picture him in this world. I'm not sure it would work. "No," I hear myself say. "It's not really a good time for you to come." I sound colder than I want to, but that's how it comes out.

"Okay, Violet," he says. "But tell me this: Are you meeting cool people up there? Do you have some friends you can talk to?"

"Of course!" I say, a little too cheerily. "I live with two great girls—Sam and Veronica—they're both super nice."

"Veronica Trask?" says Roger skeptically. "The one who trashed you in the *New York Post* today?"

"She didn't trash me," I hiss. "Besides, it's not really your business."

"Violet," he says gently, "it's in a national newspaper. It's kind of everyone's business."

I hear the lock on the door and tell Roger that I have to go. I don't wait for his response before I flip my phone shut.

Veronica walks in and drops her bag without looking at me. She heads for the bedroom. Feeling a mix of confidence and anger, I follow with the *Post* in hand.

"What is this?" I ask calmly, holding out the paper.

"Uh, looks like the *Post*," she says.

"But what is this story in here where you talk about me? When did you do this? Last night?"

"Yeah," she says nonchalantly, as she pulls her designer dress over her head and drops it on the floor. As she stands there in her bra and underwear I can see her ribs. And not just the faint outline of a few of them. But all of them. Like in detail. "After you left we may have talked to a few reporters," she says, when I continue to stare at her.

"And what did you say?"

"Well, Violet, you're the one holding the paper," she says in a tone that tells me she couldn't give a shit about this conversation. Then she pulls on a tank dress and walks out without another word to me. I hear the front door to the apartment slam shut.

My phone rings. It's my mom. I don't know what to do, but I know I can't face her right now. Even over the phone. I turn off my cell, climb into bed, and cry until I'm asleep.

*   *   *

I wake up to someone nudging my shoulder gently. "Violet," says the singsong voice.

"Mom?" I turn over in my bunk and come face-to-face with Rita. And even though it seems like the worst timing ever for her to pop in, I'm instantly glad to see her.

"Oh, Rita!" I cry. And then I really do start to cry. Again. You'd think my eyes would dry out from this flood already. But Rita just rubs my back like Mom does at home, whispering that no one else is home and I should just let it out. Eventually I quiet down.

"How about some lunch?" she says. "I know a great café near Battery Park."

As we sit by the Hudson River and watch sailboats pass and tankers float by, Rita asks me if I've heard the story of when she first moved to the city.

"Didn't you move here to get away from Grandma and Grandpa?" I ask. I think I vaguely remember that Rita came to New York when she was seventeen, but I figured she just settled in Brooklyn and has been working in mud ever since.

"Yes," she says. "But I also came to audition. I wanted to be an actress in the worst way."

"Really?" I ask.

"Really," she says, smiling. "And believe it or not, I did okay for a while. I landed a role in a well-reviewed off-Broadway play, and then I even got a few guest spots on TV."

"So why'd you stop acting?" I ask.

"Well, that's a long story," says Rita, taking a sip of her white wine. I'm having a club soda—and not just for show. After last night I feel like I don't want to drink again for a while. "The short version is that there was a point where the game wasn't about acting anymore."

"You stopped enjoying it?" I ask.

"No, I always loved the stage," Rita says. "But when it became about the hot cocktail party and the producer to be seen with and the best gossip column to be written up in so that your career would get noticed . . . well, that just wasn't for me."

I look at Rita, who has turned in my direction. "I don't know how things got so out of control with me," I say.

"Oh, Violet," she sighs. "Out of control is much worse than a little write-up in the *Post* about how sweet and innocent you are. In fact— not to sound like your agent . . . Agatha? Amelia? What's her name?"

"Angela," I say.

"Right. Well, not to sound like Angela, but that write-up will probably do you more good than harm—careerwise, anyway. But I know it's a sensitive subject."

"It is," I say, looking down at my lap but feeling better. "It's like those newspaper people write about you without thinking of you as a real person."

"Well, deep down they know you're a real person," says Rita. "But they also know that you have the benefits of being gorgeous and young and successful . . . and they present you with a price to pay for your fame."

"And for you," I say, "back when you were an actress . . . the price was too high?"

"For me, it was," she says. "But that doesn't mean my choice is right for you. You may decide that the spotlight is worth it. Maybe it's even fun?"

"Some of it is fun," I say. "It's just that you can't choose what the spotlight focuses on. You can't have it both ways."

"That's very wise, Violet," says Rita, smiling. "Just remember that, and also remember what they say about yesterday's news."

"What's that?" I ask.

"It's today's kitty-litter liner."

*　　*　　*

I think about my talk with Rita as I walk back to my apartment. I see a copy of the *Post* in the trash and I realize that what Rita said about yesterday's news is true—no one will care what was written about me as soon as there's a new boldfaced name to chatter about. I don't know why I haven't called Rita more since I've been in New York. But she hasn't called me either. Maybe she's like the superhero aunt who sweeps in only when the situation is dire. This one certainly qualified.

My cell phone rings—it's Peter. Normally I'd choose the path of avoidance, but I'm feeling strong after my talk with Rita, so I pick up.

"Hello," I say.

"Oh, hey!" he says. "I expected your voice mail."

"And why is that?" I ask.

"Well, I thought you might be—"

"Annoyed? Mad? Hurt?" I say, filling in the blanks for him. "I am."

"Listen, Violet," he says. "That reporter totally took me out of context. You know I'd never hurt you on purpose."

"No, Peter," I say. "I don't know that. I don't know you very well at all. And I don't see how 'Princess of Prude' could be taken out of context!"

"That was their ridiculous headline to draw attention," says Peter calmly. "Those were not my words."

"What about the whole 'New York eats girls like Violet for breakfast'?" I ask.

"He told me he was doing a piece on new models finding their way in the city," Peter says. "I gave him something about how hard it is to adjust to the competitive environment."

I'm silent for a minute.

"The stuff about you being sexually inexperienced?" continues Peter. "That was all from Veronica. I would never bring your personal life or our relationship into the paper like that."

It's true that the quotes about me being a virgin came from Veronica. And I guess I can see the angle of new models in the city and how a gossip-hungry reporter might have twisted his words.

"Listen," he says. "I can't stand to think you're upset. Have dinner with me tonight. No clubs, no cameras, just us. In fact, we won't even go out. Come over to my apartment and we'll get takeout."

"I don't know," I say. "I'm not sure what to think."

"Truly, Violet," Peter says. "I am so sorry they wrote something that hurt you."

I sigh.

"Come on," he says, sensing my imminent cave. "We can rent a movie—any one you want."

"Okay," I say, giving in. I want so much to believe Peter. No guy has ever taken me out before or shown so much interest in my emotions. How can I let this feeling go?

"Great!" says Peter, giving me his address. "And Violet?"

"Yes?"

"Remember: No press is bad press. See you soon, beautiful."

twenty-one

Over the next few weeks, things go well with Peter. His apartment is actually a huge loft—not a dorm at all. I imagined roommates and pizza boxes, but what I saw were Pottery Barn candles and Crate and Barrel bar sets. He's been a complete gentleman, too, never pushing me too far physically. Which means, specifically, that he's felt me up (shirtless!) but hasn't gone down below. I'm just not ready.

We've also resumed our going-out schedule, but I'm completely avoiding Veronica. She is just bad news. We still pose for pictures sometimes because the Double V thing won't die and Angela encourages me to keep up appearances, but once inside the club, we split. She spends a lot of time in the bathroom yakking up her dinner and snorting her dessert anyway.

I'm hoping to hear about the Voile job soon—Angela says it's down to just a few girls, including both me and Veronica. It would be a lot of money and a billboard in Times Square—there is nothing bigger, in every sense of the word.

My parents are coming into town this weekend. They're staying at Rita's but they want to see my apartment, which kind of worries me. I'm running around today cleaning. Sam's out of town (again) and Veronica hasn't moved from her bed yet.

Then there's a knock on the door. I've learned by now that our doorman, while adept at signing for packages, is completely ineffectual in the "announcing visitors" capacity. I'm guessing it's Peter or someone who's around a lot, so I open the door in boxers and a tank top.

"Still wearing wifebeaters on your new salary?"

It's Roger! I can't help myself—I instinctively hug him. The weird thing is, our hug lingers—and I can't tell if that's because of him or me. I realize that I haven't been this close to Roger since we were like seven years old and still had tickle fights in my family room. His shoulders feel really broad and strong—and he smells good . . . like cologne or something. When I pull away, I can feel that he's still holding on. "What are you doing here?" I ask, mentally admitting to myself that it's *really* good to see him.

"I know you said I shouldn't come, but I had to." He looks down at his shoes and I can tell he's uncomfortable, but then he perks up and grins. "Besides, my dad had a ton of frequent-flier miles he had to use up soon. And Julie's on some newspaper trip for spring break—how lame is that? I'm skipping."

"Oooh, she must be mad!" I say, smiling at the thought of Roger telling overly anal Julie that he was coming to see me instead of bonding with the newspaper staff.

"Nah, not really," he says. "She was glad I'd get to check on you. I mean, check in with you. I want to make sure you're okay."

"Why wouldn't I be?" I ask, more defensively than I mean to.

"No reason," says Roger. "I bet I'm the only guy in Chapel Hill who keeps up with New York newspapers and blogs, though. And you've been quite the cameo girl lately."

"They just like to take photos of people going out," I say. "It's no big deal."

"Right," says Roger. "Like being the entry page of Pink Is the New Blog is no big deal. But whatever . . . Hey, show me around!"

We walk into the tiny apartment and I realize that my mission to clean for my parents is in a very nascent stage. Translation: It's really messy in here.

"Hmm . . ." says Roger. "When are your parents coming?"

"Uh, tonight," I say. "Want to go to dinner with us?"

"Yes," says Roger, smiling. "But first, we need to do some damage control. Broom? Mop? Let's go."

A few hours later, the apartment is sparkling. Well, most of it. We're still waiting for sleeping Veronica to come out of her bat cave. Roger wanted to make a lot of noise to wake her up, but I advised against it. He did find her coke stash in the bathroom, and he made me swear I wasn't using any. Luckily I didn't have to lie about that.

Roger caught me up on the CHHS gossip—Shelly is still proclaiming her BFF status with me, though we haven't spoken for a few weeks. We do IM sometimes, but I don't tell Roger that—I can tell he's still annoyed that I didn't drop her last fall. When he tells me that Shelly has been talking badly about Julie, though, I feel my spine stiffen.

"What do you mean?" I ask.

"She's just saying how you dropped Julie for her, and she's been pretty vicious," he says. "She even got her henchmen to write 'Julie Evans is a LOSER' all over a bunch of copies of the newspaper last week."

I feel my eyes well up a little—it's one thing for Shelly to lie about being close with me, but another thing entirely for her to go after my best friend of like ten years. I look over at Roger, who I can tell is searching my face expectantly for a reaction. I push down the tears—that isn't my world anymore. I don't want to get wrapped up in that drama.

In a weak attempt to change the subject, I ask about Brian Radcliff, but I can't even tell if I care anymore when Roger gives me a disappointed look and tells me he's still the same old dumb jock. I mean, I don't think he's a dumb jock, but I'm not sure my crush is still as alive as it once was. Peter changed that—I think he's practically my boyfriend, but I wouldn't use that word with Roger. For some reason, I'm hesitant to tell him about Peter.

We flop down on the couch and turn on VH1.

"*Fabulous Life of . . .* marathon," I say gleefully. "Score."

"It won't be long until we're watching the *Fabulous Life of Violet Greenfield*!" says Roger.

"Oh, sure," I say. "They're already gathering B-roll."

"So how is the fabulous life?" asks Roger. "I mean, you're avoiding the cocaine but not the gossip columns—or the Cristal."

"I do drink a little," I say. "But everyone does, and it's no big deal as long as I'm not hammered. I actually think I'll be more prepared for college next year because of this alcoholic training ground." I laugh, but Roger isn't smiling. "Oh, come on, Roger, you're not going teetotaler on me, are you?"

"No," he says. "It's not that. It's just that you look . . . you look thinner. You look tired."

"Well, I'm fine," I say forcefully. I know that I am thinner, actually. A couple of proofs came back from the *Nylon* shoot and Angela said my arms looked "sausagey"—she suggested I lay off the pasta, and I have. But I still eat every day—it's not like I'm sticking the back end of a toothbrush down my throat like Veronica does. "I'm a lot more healthy than the other models I hang out with," I add.

"I'm not sure anorexic alien beings like models are a great standard to measure your own health against," says Roger. "But okay, I won't bug you. I do think that you should wear something bulky for your parents, though."

I stare at the TV screen, where the semi-British-accented voice is detailing Britney's jewelry budget. I don't look at Roger. I can't. And suddenly, I'm not sure I want him here.

Three episodes into the VH1 marathon—just as we're learning about Jay-Z's vacation houses—Veronica emerges from the bedroom. By the time the next show is on, she's been in the bathroom for forty-five minutes, but seems to have showered and even put on some makeup.

"Hi, Violet," she says. "Cheating on Heller already?"

"Nope," I say, not looking up from the TV. "I'm too prudish for that."

She sniffs in response and walks out the door.

"Was that a New York hello?" asks Roger. "Charming."

"More like a bitchy model conversation," I say. "Unfortunately, that's par for the course for us these days." I notice that Roger is staring at me from his side of the couch. "What?" I ask.

"Nothing," he says, pausing for a few seconds. "It's just that you didn't seem like you just now. You seemed sort of tough."

I'm not sure whether to take that as a compliment or not, but I just grin slightly and refocus on VH1.

A few hours later I'm still thinking about Roger's comment, and though I can't decide how I feel about him being here, my apartment does pass the parent test. We manage to avoid the bedroom by saying a roommate is sleeping in there, which—given Veronica's slumber schedule—would usually be true. The living room is pristine—glass table Windexed, magazines stacked—the kitchen is spotless, and I explain the lack of groceries by saying we order out a lot. I even show Mom my folder full of takeout menus. It's not totally untrue. I got hummus from the Middle Eastern place on the corner last night.

I'm still not happy Roger seems to be critiquing my every move, but he did help me pick out what he called a "more Carolina Violet" outfit for dinner—a light brown sweater and jeans that I haven't worn since I left home. While going through my closet, he made a lot of cracks about "model clothes," but I endured them for the sake of getting his advice on what Mom would like. I can't believe I'm as different as Roger says I am, but he keeps pointing out that "Old Violet" would never have worn three-inch heels or styled her hair with scarves, which I have to admit is true.

My parents take us to Frank, an Italian restaurant in the East Village. Dad's not really into exotic food, so I figure pasta is safe. The problem? I don't want to eat any. I keep picturing that *Nylon* shoot and Angela telling me the rigatoni was settling in my arms. I order a big salad and eat half, hoping no one will notice. Mom and Dad seem oblivious, but I see Roger scowl.

"So what's Jake doing this weekend?" I ask.

"He's got practice all week," says Dad. "But he seems happy staying home."

"More proof that sporty guys have fewer brain cells," says Roger. My parents laugh. He's been charming them since we were three, even when he's making fun of their own son.

We talk about the shoots I've done, my schedule, whether I'm sleeping enough. My parents seem genuinely happy for me to be up here. Mom actually says to me, "You're all grown up, and I'm so proud of you." Then she brings up my newspaper clips. None of my magazine shoots are out yet, so they haven't really seen anything I've done, but apparently Rita has been saving issues of the *New York Post* for them.

"Rita gave me your clippings this morning," says Mom. I forgot that they were staying in Brooklyn. I'm terrified as Mom pulls a manila folder out of her bag, but as we're flipping through the pages, I realize that Rita has done some careful editing. The photos of me and Veronica on the red carpet are all there, but none of the Page Six gossip has found its way into the pile. I make a mental note to hug Rita extra hard the next time I see her. Roger stays quiet for the most part, but as Mom puts away the folder, he smirks. "Hope she didn't miss any," he says. I glare at him.

Over dessert, Dad grills me about colleges, but it's not quite April yet, so I still don't know what my options are. I applied to UNC (of course), Vassar, and the University of Vermont, because Julie and I always had a hippie fascination with that place. I guess Julie's not a reason to go anywhere, though, considering that we haven't spoken in weeks.

I tell Mom and Dad that I'm definitely going to college next year, which seems to pacify them. But for now, I'm in New York. I'm modeling. This is my world. Mom and Dad actually seem to get that.

After dinner, my parents leave me and Roger to head back to Rita's, probably thinking we'll grab a milkshake on the corner before going home. But I have other plans, and I don't really want Roger to crash.

"Where to, city girl?" Roger asks.

"Oh, I have to help a friend get ready for a job tomorrow," I say. "She lives all the way uptown, so if you want to just go home and rest, I understand."

He looks at me in a way that says, "You're not losing me tonight." And I know he's going to come to Marquee.

*   *   *

As we pass by the huge line out front and I nod at Charles, the bouncer, on our way in, I can tell Roger's impressed. But he's trying not to be.

"Not bad, Lindsay Lohan," he whispers in my ear. "Do we get a VIP table, too?"

"But of course," I smile. I'm still annoyed that he's here, but it's fun to think that Roger might go back home and tell everyone at school that I'm a star. When we get to our table, there are lots of Tryst girls there. Peter is right in the middle of them. He scoots the two girls on his right out of the booth so he can get up to give me a kiss on the cheek. Then he turns to Roger.

"Hi, Bedford Avenue," he says, referencing the main street in Williamsburg, Brooklyn—a big hipster enclave. Roger doesn't miss a beat.

"You must be Heller's Kitchen," Roger snipes.

"Um, okay," I say. "Peter, Roger. Roger, Peter."

"Ah, a high school friend," says Peter. "Join us."

A couple girls have gotten up to dance, and Roger and I slide into their spots as Peter signals for another bottle of champagne. He pours me a glass, then asks Roger, "Does Mommy allow it?"

"Only when I'm partying with NYU boys who buy their friends," say Roger.

The night continues like this, with me in the middle. When Veronica comes to the table, she edges over to Peter and whispers something in his ear. "Excuse me," he says, as he gets up and follows her to the dance floor.

Roger and I sit silently, staring at Veronica and Peter, who've taken the floor for themselves and are dancing pretty closely. I see the other Tryst girls whispering, glancing up at me then back at Peter and Veronica. I feel Roger's presence very heavily next to me—he's seeing this too—but I don't want to acknowledge anything. Why can't he just observe a perfectly glamorous evening? Why does he have to be here for *this*?

"Uh, Violet," he says. "You wanna go home?"

"No," I snap, pouring myself another glass of champagne. I don't look at him, but I can tell he's looking at me. I can feel his eyes. And I know the emotion behind them: pity. "Look, Roger, why don't you just get out of here!" I yell. I'm surprised at my own volume but I don't stop. "I didn't ask you to come, and I don't need you to 'check up on me.' " I actually use air quotes for that phrase, which Roger and I once pledged we'd never do.

"Violet, look, I'm just trying to—" Roger starts. But I cut him off. I can't stand to hear any more of his judgmental crap. I stand up and stare down at him.

"I am FINE!" I shout. "The press loves me. I have fans and photographers who request me. ME! And I have a great boyfriend who cares about how I feel."

"Oh, really?" says Roger. "You mean the one who's grinding Veronica Trask on the dance floor right now?"

I turn to see the dancing scene, and it's true. But it's just dancing. "You have no idea what this world is like," I say to him. "You sit in North Carolina scrolling through Gawker and Fishbowl and thinking that you're a part of things. Well, you're not. You're just a sad, sad nerd of a boy who fills his time reading about other people's lives because he doesn't have one of his own. Go back to your blogs. Hey, maybe you'll even make the *Post* tomorrow—in the background of a photo of *me*."

"I don't know much about this world?" screams Roger. "Maybe that's true. But I know how to treat my friends and people I care about. And I know that if I were that Peter douchebag, I'd sure as hell be thanking my lucky stars that I could be by your side all night and not on the floor with that coked-up line drawing of a girl. Keys!"

"Huh?" I say.

"Give me your keys," Roger says. "I'm going home. Believe me, if I were an adult who could afford a hotel, this would be a much cooler exit scene because I wouldn't have to ask for your keys."

I smile a little then, but Roger isn't having it. I hand him my keys and he storms out, leaving me alone in a booth to watch my boyfriend dance with my nemesis.

twenty-two

I wake up with a headache. Again. Veronica isn't in her bed and Sam is still traveling. I feel grateful to be alone in the apartment so I can sleep and laze around today—I don't think I have any appointments. Maybe I'll airpop some popcorn and watch a movie—I recorded *13 Going on 30* on DVR.

And then I remember. Roger's here. And we had a big fight.

I will myself to get out of bed, and I pull the sheets from my bunk with me as I walk out into the living room. I'm wearing pajamas but I don't feel like getting dressed yet, so Roger can deal with me sheet-wrapped. Once he makes fun of my hair a little bit and teases me about being lazy, things will be okay. He'll forget that I yelled at him last night and he stormed out of Marquee to sleep on my futon during his last night of spring break.

But when I shuffle into the living room, Roger's not there. A blanket is neatly folded atop the pillow he borrowed from Sam. And there's a note.

Dear Violet,

*Thank you for letting me stay on your "couch." I'm glad
everything is "fine" here and you're doing "well." Have fun.*

Your "Pal,"

Roger

Leave it to Roger to mock my use of air quotes last night in print
form. The tone seems sarcastic but not overly angry, which makes
me feel relieved. Then I see the P.S.

*P.S. You might want to take the time to eat a little more, drink a
little less, make some real friends, and get some help for that
powder-snorting bulimic you live with. The old Violet would be
alarmed—are you?*

I crumple up the paper and toss it toward the wastebasket as my
eyes fill with tears. How dare he tell me how I'm supposed to feel
about my own life!

I sniffle for a little while as I settle into a *Cribs* marathon. MTV has
covered so many celebrities that they're now on a major D-list run—
like the drummer from No Doubt and other people I barely recognize.
Maybe that's why it's so easy for me to tune out and let Roger's words
ring in my head. I pull up my tank top and look down at my stomach.
I can see my ribs pretty clearly. Am I getting thinner? I hold up my arm
and pinch the bottom part—the pasta jiggle that Angela pointed out.
But my arms are kind of sticks—they always have been. I decide to
order some Chinese food—chicken with mixed vegetables. It's not totally unhealthy, but it's more of a greasefest than I've had in weeks.

While I'm scarfing down the last bit of rice, Veronica walks in.
She looks dead on her feet, but somehow even run down, she's got
an ethereal glow. She smiles at me wickedly. "I got the Voile campaign," she says. "Angela just told me."

My heart sinks a little bit—that would have been a huge break for me. But I squelch my remorse and smile. "That's great, Veronica," I say, feeling generous (and also, I admit, wanting to have a real friend here—the friend I once thought Veronica might be). "Want to go get ice cream by the river to celebrate?"

Veronica glares at me. "No, Pollyanna, I do not want to go get ice cream by the river!" she snaps. "Don't pretend like you're happy for me. You're just waiting to get your little claws on every job I have."

My eyes widen. "What?" I say meekly. "No, Veronica, I . . ."

But she's already down the hall, slamming the bathroom door shut. I sit on the couch, stunned and full of brown rice. Veronica should be really happy—this job is insanely high profile, and I know for a fact they're paying big money for it. It will probably get her more magazine covers—Angela told me she's kind of hit a lull over the past few months. It will mean the comeback of her name, too. So why is she so angry? And more than that—why is she so sad?

I start to think about all of the times we had fun together—or so I thought—and how at one point I genuinely cared about Veronica. And then I go over the things she's done to hurt me—from the *Post* story to angling for Peter to subtly sabotaging me at shoots and go-sees. And I realize that no matter what is going on for her—red carpets or magazine shoots or dancing at Marquee or walking in from a late night—she always has a deep, dark sadness in her eyes. At first I thought it was part of her look—the brooding, moody model face. But she wore it even when we were out shopping and laughing. She never loses it. I feel an unexpected surge of sympathy for Veronica, and I go to the bathroom door.

"Knock, knock," I say, as I tap softly on the door. I push it gently, expecting it to be locked. It swings open slightly.

I can see Veronica on her knees, leaning over the bowl. She's holding her hair back with one hand as she jams the back end of a toothbrush down her throat with the other. Then I hear the noise. *Buuuuleeeech.* I cringe and step back instinctively. Veronica turns and looks up. There's a little drop of blood at the corner of her nose, and her soft brown eyes are rimmed in red.

"Get out of here, you fucking bitch!" she screams, pawing at the door to try to close it. Every ounce of the old me wants to step back, sit down on the futon, and turn up the volume on *Cribs*. But Roger's right. I have changed.

I step forward and jam my foot in the door so Veronica can't close it. I grab the toothbrush from her hand and pull some toilet paper off the roll. "Stand up," I say in a voice so solid and strong that I hardly recognize it as my own. She looks at me, shocked and then furious. "I said get out of here!" she shrieks. "I hate you!"

She does stand up now, but it's to lunge at me. She tries to grab my hair, but I push her up against the wall. She's so frail that it's not hard even for me to hold her still. Veronica is writhing and gnashing her teeth, and it reminds me of a crazy Lifetime movie where the daughter has to physically contain her alcoholic mother. After a minute of spitting at me and screaming, "I hate you!" over and over, Veronica goes limp. I take the toilet paper and wipe the blood from her nose as I smooth back her hair. "Stay still," I whisper, running a washcloth under the tap and then using it to cool down her face, which is covered in sweat from her efforts.

It's then, as I'm slowly running the cloth over her face, that she starts to cry. She slides down the wall of the bathroom and into a tight ball. I don't know what else to do, so I slide down with her and put my arm around her shoulders. Eventually she looks up. "I'm okay," she says. "I just want to sleep." I help her stand up and she walks into our room and closes the door.

I want to go in and talk to her, make sure she's all right, but I feel like we've had our bizarre Hallmark moment for today. I sit back down in the living room and flip through *New York* magazine, not really reading anything. Fifteen minutes pass and I can't stand the quiet, so I go into the bedroom to check on Veronica. She's sprawled out on her bed, sleeping. But there's something about her pose, about the way her arms are flung to the sides, that makes me nervous. I shake her shoulder and say her name. She doesn't respond. I push her harder, until her head moves to the other side of the pillow, but she doesn't wake up.

I call Angela. She'll know what to do. Once we've gotten past the "darlings," I interrupt her explanation of why Veronica got the Voile campaign.

"Angela, I can't wake her up," I say. "Her nose was bleeding and she was throwing up in the toilet and then she said she needed to sleep but now I'm shaking her and I can't wake her up!"

"Violet, slow down," says Angela, dropping her usual purr. "Are you talking about Veronica?"

"Yes!" I yell.

"I'll call an ambulance," she says. "You stay right there. I'm over in five."

The rest of the afternoon is a blur. EMTs, Angela screaming to get Veronica a private room at the hospital, and—worst of all—Veronica waking up on a stretcher as they wheel her out of the apartment. It's all hazy except for what she screamed. "I hate you, Violet Greenfield! You are *not* me! You will not take my place!"

I spend the rest of the day crying softly on the couch, and when my mother calls that night to tell me they got home safely, I don't dare answer the phone.

twenty-three

Without Veronica in the house, I'm inside my head a lot. Because Veronica is "dehydrated and exhausted," as people like to euphemize, the Voile campaign went to the next girl in line—me. Angela was thrilled down to her French pedicure, but I could hardly summon a smile when I heard the news. I'm not sure any of this matters to me anymore. I got letters from Carolina, Vassar, and UVM—all three took me. Dad was giddy, and told me he thought my modeling experience put me over the top. I just feel numb.

Sam is still in and out of town, and a new girl named Casey moved into the one empty bed—I wouldn't let her take Veronica's even though it's unclear when she'll be back. Casey's very upbeat and has that blond, freckled, cornfed look to her—she's from Kansas. She goes on castings with such excitement and hope in her eyes that I want to hug her and pack her suitcase to send her home. Sometimes at night she'll sit on the couch with me and watch TV. I can tell she's eager to talk, but I keep a blank face so she won't get too chatty.

We're sitting on the futon together now, watching *The Cosby Show* on Nick at Nite. Instead of following Theo and Cockroach's exploits, though, I'm pulling at a thread in our knit blanket, which I have wrapped around me semipermanently these days. I can't seem to stay warm. I'm thinking about how I haven't seen Peter much lately. I haven't been to a club since Veronica got sick. And I haven't heard from Roger or Julie. My conversations with my parents are more and more superficial. I find myself practicing a cheery voice before I return their calls, if I return them at all.

Suddenly Casey says, "Violet, I think you have the most wonderful air about you."

"What do you mean?" I ask, turning toward her without a hint of a smile.

"You're very poised," she says, straightening her posture to imitate me, I suppose. "You move slowly and gracefully, and even when you're slouching you make it look engaging and lovely."

I want to tell her that I move slowly because I'm in a fog. Because the girl who used to sleep in the bunk below her is in a hospital up in Harrison, New York. Because every time I book a shoot I dull my ears so I won't hear the critiques of my body and face. And my mouth has turned into a permanent straight line because although my *Teen Girl* pages came out and I'm getting IMed and texted and e-mailed and MySpaced by everyone in my high school, the two people who matter most haven't reached out at all. But I'm just not ready to discuss this all with Cornfed Casey. I don't want to get into what's happening with me or where Veronica went or why modeling isn't what I thought.

So I just smile slightly and turn back to the TV, sinking deeper into the feeling that I have no friends and no one to really talk to. And then I think about Veronica. She's upstate, alone, and all I've done is sign an agency card that went with her flowers. I grab my cell and call Angela. It's past work hours but she's never off duty, I know.

"Violet," she coos. "The Voile shoot is going to be gorgeous— we just booked Mario Testino." It's weird to me that I know what she means by that—he's a famous photographer who shoots for *Vogue*. This is the kind of thing that fills my head now.

"Angela, I want to go see Veronica," I say.

"Oh, darling, we sent flowers and that was gorgeous of us," she says. "Don't worry about visiting. You've got castings to think about."

"I want to cancel everything for tomorrow," I say. "I need to see her." I'm surprised to hear the firmness in my voice—inside I'm quaking with emotion. It works, though.

"I'll call Mario," says Angela quietly. "He'll drive you."

After I get off the phone with Angela, I turn to Casey.

"Will you help me get ready for a date?" I ask.

I haven't seen Peter in a while. He walked around Central Park with me the day after Veronica went into the hospital, but he seemed kind of distant. Still, he's been texting me every day and checking in. And he's coming over tonight to take me to dinner.

Casey looks up at me with total joy. What's funny is that she's the kind of classically pretty girl who would have completely intimidated me just last summer. But, like many things this year, my perceptions have changed. Casey is over the moon when I ask to borrow a flowery cotton button-down she brought from home. I show her how, with a leather belt and a pencil skirt underneath, it looks more Tocca runway than Kansas wheat field.

Peter knocks promptly at eight P.M., and he kisses my cheek

when I open the door. Then he edges past me and takes Casey's hand to plant a kiss there. "Miss Casey, looking lovely," he says. She turns red and giggles. *Was that me six months ago?*

"See you later," I say to Casey, as we head out the door.

"She seems sweet," says Peter. I give him a hmph.

We go to Nobu, where Peter has a table reserved. I haven't been here since the day Angela took me and Mom to dinner right after I got my new glasses and the clothes at Bendel's. It feels like a hundred years ago.

As we sit down and order our appetizers, we talk about the Voile campaign, and Peter goes on and on about how my career will really take off after this break. He knows—he watched it happen with Veronica after she landed an Estée Lauder gig. "It was fantastic!" he says. "Veronica was on top of the world." He doesn't mention her current "dehydration."

"I'm going to see Veronica tomorrow," I say.

"Why?" says Peter, looking around the restaurant and hardly paying attention to me. I realize he does that a lot—he stares over my shoulder to see who else might walk in.

"Because she's alone," I say.

"You don't know that," says Peter, finally meeting my eyes. "For all we know her extended family is visiting her every day. I think they're from Connecticut."

"That's the thing, though," I say. "We don't know. We hardly know a thing about Veronica. And I just get the feeling that she's alone."

Peter shrugs.

"Do you want to come with me?" I ask, realizing that this is a big question. It may be the most important question I've ever asked Peter, and his response carries more weight with me than he could know.

He's quiet for a minute, and he puts his fork down as he takes a sip of water. I'm staring at him intently, and when he looks up at me he says, "Huh? What? Did you ask me something?"

"I asked if you wanted to go with me," I repeat. Chance number two.

"To see Veronica?" he says. "Oh, God no, Violet. Visiting people in rehab is just tacky."

I get through the rest of dinner somehow and let him walk me home. "Good-bye, Peter," I say at the door. He tries to kiss my cheek but I move out of the way. I can tell by his wave that he doesn't much care that I said good-bye and not good night.

When I get into the car with Mario the next day, it feels like a reunion. "Violet!" he yells, leaning over the seat to give me a kiss on the cheek. And then I wonder why I got into the backseat. I move up front next to Mario.

At first, neither of us says much. Mario asks me about what jobs I've been doing; I ask him about his family. He knows exactly where we're going, so I know he sees through all the "Oh, yes, photo shoots are so exciting!" talk I give him. But it's not until we get past the city traffic, out into the countryside—which is surprisingly close to Manhattan—that he breaches anything deeper.

"You look different, Violet," he says.

"I know," I sigh, feeling defensive. "I've changed. I'm not as bright-eyed, I look tired, I'm thinner. I've heard it."

"No, no," says Mario. "You look stronger."

I let that sit with me for a few minutes. Who would have ever thought that Violet Greenfield would be someone who looked *strong*? Over the past few months I've come to think of myself as possibly pretty, maybe more independent, perhaps even a little more confident—but the word *strong* never entered my mind.

When I leave the safety of Mario's Town Car to enter the doors of St. Vincent's Harrison outpost, though, I'm hoping he's right.

"I'm here to see Veronica Trask," I tell the receptionist, a sweet-looking old woman with square-framed glasses.

"Oh good!" she says, clasping her hands together and smiling. "Dear Miss Trask hasn't had a single visitor. I was starting to get worried. Are you a relative?"

"No," I say. "Just a . . . um, friend."

"Well, sign in here," she says, handing me a clipboard. "I'll get an aide to take you down."

This place is no joke. I follow a very tall, very broad man down the stark white hallway. Veronica's room is at the end of a corridor. It's actually bigger than our room at home—and it's all hers. No bunks, just a twin bed by the window with a blue cotton comforter. Veronica is turned to the window, so I can't tell if she's asleep. The aide leaves me there, and I walk up to her bed slowly.

"Veronica?" I whisper. "Are you awake?"

"Violet!" She sits right up in bed. "Jesus, this place is so fucking boring I think I'm starting to hallucinate. Are you actually there?"

"Yes," I say. "Totally! I came to see you." I sound fake cheery, but Veronica doesn't seem to notice. I look around the room, and I'm so glad to see a table covered with bouquets. They're wilted and dying, but still. I walk over and glance at a few cards. Most are pretty generic—"Get Well Soon" and "Best Wishes" type messages. Whenever I sign a group card, I try really hard to write something semipersonal—I'll recall a private joke or an anecdote, just so the person knows I didn't just scribble something automatic. Most people aren't like that, though.

"It's like I died the way they keep pushing flowers on me," says Veronica. "Oh, check out the perfect peonies from *Vogue*. They always have to be different."

"It's nice that everyone took the time to send something," I say, noticing orange tiger lilies from the *Nylon* staff and purple irises from *Elle*. There are even yellow daisies from Stella McCartney because Veronica always walks her runway show.

"Those flowers are my exit cue," says Veronica. "They're the, 'Oh, she's coked out and bulimic' death knell."

"I'm sure that's not true," I say, pulling up an overstuffed chair from the corner so I can sit close to Veronica's bed.

"It is," Veronica sighs. "Only Kate Moss can come back after the EMTs are at the door."

Despite Angela's efforts to block cameras, the press did get some photos of Veronica being carried out of our apartment building. She wasn't front page the next day, but her eating disorder and drug use have gotten some press. Enough for insiders to notice, anyway.

"I heard you got Voile," she says. I've been afraid of her knowing that, but she doesn't sound angry.

"Yeah," I say, looking down.

"Hey, if it can't be me, I'm glad it's you," she says. And she sounds like she really means it. I think about how scary Veronica was when I first met her. Actually, it's not like the cold stares ever really let up, but looking at her now, she seems so meek and fragile. And abandoned.

"Can I ask you something?" I say.

"Sure," she says, leaning back on her pillow. "What's up?"

"Well, it's just that . . ." I start. I'm having trouble being direct because she still really does intimidate me, but then I think of what Mario said about how I've changed. "I wonder if we could ever be friends. Because I liked it when I thought we were."

I hear her exhale slowly, but she doesn't speak, so I go on.

"I know you feel competitive with me, but I never set out to be at your level," I say. "I would never even dream that I would be capable of standing in your shoes—let alone stealing them from you entirely."

"I know," says Veronica slowly.

"But then why—?" I start.

"That's just it," says Veronica. "You were so unassuming and 'fresh'—God, I hate it when Angela uses that word—and you made me feel like a used-up old hag with too much eye makeup on."

"But you're so beautiful and successful," I say.

"So are you, Violet," says Veronica, looking at me for the first time since I started the awkward talk. "And you're also a good person. I think we'll both agree that you've got that over me by a mile."

I smile a little.

"Listen," she continues. "It means a lot to me that you came up here. No one's really visited me."

"So the receptionist told me," I say.

"Oh, great," says Veronica, rolling her eyes. "I'm going to have to put her on the payroll to keep her quiet so I don't seem like a total loser."

We both laugh.

"What I'm trying to say," Veronica continues, "is that I'm sorry for the *Post* article. And for all the go-see tricks. And for trying to make you jealous with Peter—who, by the way, is so not good enough for you."

"Oh, I found that out," I say, thinking of how this visit is the complete opposite of tacky, like Peter said.

"I knew you would," says Veronica. "You're a smart girl."

We stop talking then, and I feel like both of us know that there's something between us. Something like real friendship.

We spend the next few minutes talking about how Veronica hates the food here—but she is eating it—and how she should be out in a few weeks. "I'm like an ideal patient," she says. "Out here in the country with the crazies, I'm the normal girl."

Soon, I stand up to go.

"It's good to see you, V," I say.

"Thanks, Double V," says Veronica. "And hey—kick some ass at the Voile shoot for me."

"I will," I reply, knowing even as I say it that I won't be at that shoot. "I'm practicing my evil Veronica stare."

"Hey, that's a patented look," she says, winking at me as I walk out the door, feeling pretty damn strong.

twenty-four

When I get back to the apartment, I take out my suitcase and start folding my clothes. Sam is at home—for once—and she sits on the bunk across from mine with a half smile on her face.

"Done?" she asks.

"I think so," I say. "For now, anyway."

"Don't let Page Six forget your name, Violet," she says. "They're not kind to has-beens."

"I appreciate the advice," I say. "But better a has-been model than a has-been me."

Sam cocks an eyebrow then and says, "I thought you had more ambition than that."

I smile. "Maybe this just isn't my dream," I say. And then I walk out the door. Mario's waiting on the street, and he helps me load my bags into the trunk.

"Brooklyn?" he asks.

"Brooklyn," I say.

When I arrive on Rita's porch, I wait a few minutes before ringing her buzzer. I remember the first day I sat out here in the sun with my things. I was hoping for so much—romance, adventure, glamour. I guess I got what I wished for—one way or another.

Rita pokes her head out the screen door. She's wearing a floppy straw sun hat and clay-splattered overalls. "Hey, kid," she says, glancing down at my suitcase. "Raggedy Ann is getting lonely downstairs." I stand up from the stoop and give her a big hug. She doesn't let go for a few seconds and neither do I.

We head inside and she starts fixing peanut butter and jelly sandwiches. I sit on a stool in her kitchen, like I'm five, and watch her intently.

"Something happen in the house?" she asks, still jellying the white bread.

"You could say that," I respond.

"Anything to do with that Veronica stuff I read in the paper?"

"Sort of," I say.

I'm silent for another minute as she finishes cutting our sandwiches diagonally. She hands me mine, wrapped in a paper towel. "Let's eat in the garden," she says.

We go downstairs and out back. I'm so grateful to have a private outdoor space—something I completely took for granted at home. I hadn't realized how boxed-in that model apartment could get.

"So did you tell Angela you were leaving?" asks Rita.

"Not yet," I say. "She'll freak."

"Probably," says Rita. "Do you care?"

"I don't know," I say. Suddenly the strong feeling has left me, and I'm wondering what I'm doing in this backyard in Brooklyn with PB&J when I should be booking photo shoots and signing a Voile contract. Shouldn't I?

"Hmph," snorts Rita. "What *do* you know, Violet?" She says it in a nice way, like she's really asking me to think about it.

I know that I felt a lot more solid at home, I think. *Even with my bad posture and wiry glasses. I know that Angela and Peter congratulating me on landing jobs and being a boldfaced name and losing an eighth of an inch on my arms doesn't feel nearly as good as when I hear that stupid brass dinner bell ring at six thirty P.M. I know that I'd rather be in the beat-up old Rabbit with Julie and Roger heading to Carolina Beach for the weekend than riding in a Voile limo on the way to shoot a billboard.*

"I think I wanna go home," I say.

Rita smiles. "For good?" she asks.

"For now," I say.

"Not a bad idea," she says. "Seems like there might be some people there who'd love to hear from you."

"I've been talking to Mom like twice a week," I say defensively.

"You've been calling her, I'm sure," says Rita. "But we both know you haven't *really* been talking to her."

I shrug, but I know that Rita's right.

"Well, you know where the phone is," Rita says, turning to her garden and bending over to grab a weed. I guess that's the signal that this conversation is over. I go inside and dial home.

Calling Mom and Dad to tell them I was coming home was easy. In fact, they sounded really happy that I'd be back, and they didn't press me for information about why I want a break. Yet.

Calling Angela, however, wasn't exactly pleasant.

"What do you mean, North Carolina?" she snapped, when I mentioned I'd gotten myself a ticket.

"You know, where I'm from," I said. "I just need to go home for a while."

"Not possible," she told me. "You've got the Voile shoot next week."

"Well, I haven't signed the contract yet," I said, feeling bold. "And I'm just not sure—"

"Not sure about what?" Angela interrupted. "Not sure that you want your face all over New York City, not to mention on ad pages in every influential magazine in the world? Not sure that you want to become an international superstar? Not sure that you want to take a job any girl would kill to have?"

"Yeah," I replied. "I'm just not sure."

"Well, Violet, I'll tell you what I'm sure about," says Angela, in a dark tone I haven't heard from her before. "I'm sure that if you leave this city without my permission, I will drop you like Brad dropped Jennifer when Angelina came to town."

I expected that, and I was ready. I said, "I know. I'm going anyway."

Then I did something that I learned from Angela: I hung up without waiting for a response.

On my first night home, Dad cooks burgers while Mom sits in the dining room reading a book about early childhood development. Jake gave me a fast hug and a head nod before retreating to his room when he got home from practice. I'm not sure how to interpret that, but at least I didn't get ignored completely, which I might deserve after being so out of touch. My parents are easy, though. I gave them the "I was so busy with shoots" line when they chided me for not calling enough, and they're excited about my spread in *Teen Girl*, so they just beamed at my work ethic. They actually have about ten copies of the magazine in the living room spread out over the coffee table. "Sweet overkill," I said when I saw them.

I've been avoiding calls from Angela, and I know it won't be long until she calls Mom directly, so I have to have a talk with my parents. But I can't stop thinking about setting things right with Julie and Roger, too. I'm ready to get my life back.

When Dad rings the dinner bell, I'm already helping him bring out the burgers. I figure tonight isn't a good night to sulk in my room—I did enough of that on the model-apartment futon. Besides, I'm the one who wants to have the real conversation this evening.

"Isn't it great to have your big sis home?" Dad says to Jake, who's pulling his iPod headphones from his ears.

"What? Oh yeah," says Jake. He smiles at me.

"Violet, it's so nice that you got some time off to visit," says Mom. I haven't exactly told them that I don't have a return ticket. I didn't lie, just left that part out.

"Actually, Mom," I start. "I've been wanting to talk to you about that."

"You'll be here for the week at least?" asks Dad.

"Uh, yeah," I say. "I'll be here for the summer."

"All summer?" says Jake, perking up from his burger binge.

"Well, until college starts," I say. "Then I guess I'll move into the dorms."

Mom looks a little dumbfounded. "Did something go wrong, Violet? Did Angela kick you out?"

"I kicked myself out," I say.

"What do you mean?" asks Mom. "I thought you were getting work—didn't you just land a job for some big designer? Chartreuse or something?"

"Voile." I laugh. "But I don't think I'll be welcome on that shoot after telling Angela I was leaving New York."

"Weren't you doing well, Violet?" asks Dad.

"I was," I say. "I mean, I was doing well in their terms. I booked a lot of shoots and I was making money, if that's what you're talking about."

"Yeah," says Jake. "I saw your savings account balance, money-bags."

"It's true," I say. "Modeling is lucrative. I'll need that money for college, though, right, Dad?"

"Sure, honey," he says. "If that's what you want."

"It is," I say.

"So it simply wasn't for you?" says Mom, still confused. "Just like that?"

"Mom, don't give me a lot of shit," I say, getting annoyed.

"Violet," says my father in that deeper voice that says *Watch it*.

"Sorry, but this is my decision," I say. "And I would think you'd be happy that I'm home."

"Oh, sweetie, we are," says Mom, softening. "It's just that this seems sudden, and you're not giving us much of an explanation."

"You want an explanation?" I say, getting worked up. "Fine. Here goes: I felt like Tryst was using me, I had no friends, the guy I was dating sold me out for flashbulbs and red-carpet moments, I was treated like an inanimate doll at photo shoots, and my roommate had a cocaine problem and an eating disorder. Is that good enough?"

The table falls silent until my brother says, "Whoa."

"Violet, are you in trouble?" says Dad. Mom looks like she's on the verge of tears.

"No, you guys," I say, realizing that I might have just given them a little TMI. "I just wanted to come home. I want to be me again. Even if being me means that I'm not the prettiest or the most excit-ing girl, and no one at school talks to me except for Roger and Julie."

"Violet, that's never how it was for you," says Mom. "You've al-ways been special."

I smile at both of my parents, and my brother, feeling happy to just be at home. But there's something I need to take care of here.

"Can I be excused?" I ask.

"I don't think we're done talking about this," says Mom. "I'll have to call Angela and see what's in your contract—I know it was going to be up in mid-May, but I'll have to check on any jobs you're committed to and if there's—"

"I know," I say, interrupting the conveyor belt of anxiety that's emerging from my mom's mouth. "I swear we can talk tomorrow. But there's something I have to do tonight. Can I borrow the car?" I look over at my dad, and he hands me the keys without any questions. I kiss him on the cheek and say, "Julie's."

He looks back at me and winks. "I know," he says. Which means I may be in more trouble with her than I thought.

twenty-five

As I drive over to Julie's, I'm still not sure what I'm going to say to her. We haven't spoken in about two months, and our last conversation consisted of her telling me she thought I was losing myself and me retorting that I didn't have time to talk—I had to get ready to go out. That was when I was first getting swept up in the Veronica wave. Just remembering it makes me cringe.

I'm so used to just opening up her side door and walking in that it feels funny going to the front—only strangers ring the bell. I didn't want to call first in case Julie told me not to come over, but now I'm nervous that she'll think I'm bamboozling her into talking to me. Which I guess I am.

Through the glass side panel, I see Julie's mom coming to the door.

"Violet!" says Mrs. Evans. "I thought you were in New York!"

"I was," I say, "but I'm back now."

She smiles with her lips closed, which always seems disingenuous to me.

"Is she home?" I ask, looking past Mrs. Evans into the foyer.

"Oh, of course, come in!" she says.

As I start to step inside the house, I see Julie coming down the hall. She must have heard my voice because she's carrying a small box, and I can see an old sweatshirt of mine from junior high hanging over one edge. Before I even come in, Julie's standing in front of me, blocking the way.

Mrs. Evans turns and walks away.

"Here," Julie says to me, handing over the box. Then she starts to turn around.

"Julie, I came over to—"

She swings back to face me. "I don't care what you came over to say, Violet. It's very clear that we're no longer friends, so let's just move on."

My throat clenches up, and I can tell that in another ten seconds my eyes will flood with tears. But Julie is already down the hall.

"I wanted to say I'm sorry," I say. I see her pause for a tiny beat, but then she keeps walking. I take my box, get back in the car, and start to cry.

When I get home, I avoid my parents and go straight to my room. I log on to IM, but though Roger and Julie are both online, the only person who IMs me is Shelly. She thinks I'm still in New York, where I was hardly ever online, so she takes this opportunity to ask me about representation, her chances, what the designers are really like—*again*. I guess it's my fault for ever indulging her friendship. Hard to believe that less than a year ago, being friends with Shelly Ryan was one of my goals.

Now my goal list would look like this:

1. Get my old life back.

I don't have the nerve to IM Julie right now, but I type a quick "Hi" to Roger and hit Send before I chicken out.

RC1: Hi.
VIOLET GREENFIELD: i'm back
RC1: Is that a Poltergeist reference?
VIOLET GREENFIELD: no. i'm really back
RC1: In CH?
VIOLET GREENFIELD: yes
RC1: Oh. How long?
VIOLET GREENFIELD: for good, I think
RC1: No more cokehead roommate or A-hole boyfriend?
VIOLET GREENFIELD: long story, but no
VIOLET GREENFIELD: and i'm so sorry about everything
RC1: Does Julie know you're back?
VIOLET GREENFIELD: uh, yeah
RC1: I'm guessing that didn't go well.
VIOLET GREENFIELD: nope
RC1: Are you back wearing high-heeled boots and shopping
    with ShellBelle until the fall shows, or are you really back?
VIOLET GREENFIELD: i'm really back
VIOLET GREENFIELD: i hope
RC1: Give Julie a few days. I'll call you tomorrow.
VIOLET GREENFIELD: hey, roger?
RC1: That's Rivers to you.
VIOLET GREENFIELD: haha.
VIOLET GREENFIELD: well thanks, rivers
RC1: Always for you, superstar.

I fall asleep holding the sweatshirt that Julie returned. At least I have one best friend who's still with me.

*   *   *

I let a few days go by without pushing Julie. Roger and I are meeting for dinner tonight in Durham at the Cosmic Cantina on Ninth Street. We never go to Durham, but he's getting all 007 on me and says he can't be seen with me around Chapel Hill. I agree, but only because I don't want to run into the BK. Shelly heard that I'm back and she's been calling me nonstop. I programmed a special ring for Shelly and Angela—Carly Simon's "You're So Vain"—and when it plays, guaranteed I'm not picking up.

"Hey you," says Roger, as he slides into the booth across from me.

I smile. He's wearing a white shirt that says NYU. "Are you trying to break some news with that shirt?" I ask.

"Just the news that I'm the hippest high school kid round these parts," he says, in a cowboy drawl. "Oh, and that I got into NYU."

"No way!" I scream, "That's amazing!" I stand up to hug him across the table. It's kind of awkward, but again I feel his broad shoulders and realize that Roger's actually like a guy now.

When we pull apart, he's staring at me intently—I've hardly ever noticed how blue his eyes are behind those dark frames. "Well, I thought you'd be there," says Roger. "That made it even more of a dream school for me."

I actually blush a little bit, which is so weird because—*hello!*—it's Roger. "I call bullshit," I say, wanting to break the bizarrely awkward moment we're having. "You've been talking about NYU since preschool."

"Yeah, well . . ." says Roger, trailing off. "Anyway, I've been working on Miss Evans to give up her dreams of Brown for Columbia or NYU, and I think she's caving a bit."

"Really?" I ask, thinking how ironic it would be if Julie and Roger both ended up in the city that I just left—possibly for good.

"She seemed so angry when I saw her," I say. "I mean like 'I could take on Naomi Campbell right now' angry."

"Look at you with your supermodel refs." Roger laughs. "But seriously, no one can take Naomi without a weapon."

"Semantics," I say, "but you see my point."

"I do," says Roger. "And I'm not saying she's not still angry. She is. And, honestly, so am I." He looks at me hard. "You ditched us, Violet."

"I know," I say. "But I was so busy with work up there—you don't know what the pressure is like. I was—"

"Stop," says Roger, interrupting. "I really don't want to hear it. I was there, remember? I know what it was like. You could have made time for us. You just wanted to be the new you—the one who didn't have two old best friends who reminded you of the days when you weren't Violet Greenfield, Supermodel."

You're right, I think. I can't get myself to say it, though. I look at Roger pleadingly.

"Lucky for you, I'm a forgiver," he says.

"I know," I say, smiling gratefully. "And Julie?"

"Eh, not so much," says Roger. "But for you, she might fold her guilt cards. She knows she's got you on the ropes, Violet."

"I'll make it up to you guys," I say.

"You sure will," says Roger. "Oh, hey, do you have plans Saturday night?"

"I don't have any plans ever," I say, laughing. "It's so weird not being in school during the day. I'm starting on Carolina's summer reading list."

"Nerd," says Roger.

"Look who's talking!" I reply.

"Touché," he says. "Anyway, save the date."

"Why?"

"Questions later!" he shouts, raising his hand in the air to call the waiter over. "Right now I just want some freaking salsa! Let's order."

twenty-six

Saturday feels like every other day to me now that I'm just hanging out at home. Dad has taken to calling me "Paris Hilton" because I'm not working at all. I argue that I earned my money this spring—I have enough now to help pay for college, or to pay for all of my first year if I go to Carolina, which has really cheap in-state tuition. I just can't decide about college right now. Or anything. I should be able to relax, but I'm going stir crazy. I might pick up a shift at the theater, but when I went over there to see Richard, he asked me so many questions about New York that I was overwhelmed and decided that working the candy shelves might be harder than it used to be with a starstruck manager at my side. Still, it was nice to see Benny, who squinted his eyes and smiled as he asked, "Did you get to meet any rock stars, man?" I told him that I did run into Mick Jagger one night at Bungalow 8, and Benny told me that even *he* was jealous of me now.

I'm lying on the couch watching *Point Break*, which is a movie

I've seen ten times but can always get into, when my brother walks in with a big dry-cleaning bag.

"What's that?" I ask.

"Tux," Jake says.

"What for?"

"Duh, Violet," he says. "The prom."

I forgot completely about the prom! "Oh," I say, trying to seem nonchalant. Jake's already upstairs. A thousand thoughts run through my head: *Should I go? Is this why Roger asked me to save Saturday night? Is he taking me? Will everyone at school snub me?*

I race to my room and throw open my closet doors. *Would it be obnoxious to wear a designer gown to prom?* Then I get an idea. I grab the cerulean blue, strapless silk Nicholas Gravisi gown that I kept from the *Nylon* shoot. It has an amazing hourglass shape to it because the waist is nipped in by a dark red ribbon. The editor said the designer himself requested that I take it. Of course, then I wore it out that weekend and it got into the *Post* and he got all kinds of publicity, which is how one hand washes the other. But still. It's worth like thousands of dollars. And Julie looks gorgeous in blue.

I rifle through my desk drawers to find a specific yellow Post-it note. For once, my habit of never throwing things out is coming in handy. Last year, Julie was a bridesmaid in her cousin's wedding, and we used a tape measure of mine to determine her bust, waist, hips, and height inches. Found it!

I grab Dad's keys without asking and run to the car. There's a tailor near the theater, and I'm hoping she's not too busy.

When I get to the shop, she's swamped. "I have extra staff here today," she snaps at me. "It's prom day! I cannot fit something on the day of! She must come in, try on—"

"Please!" I say, pressing my hands together like I'm praying to her. "I need this dress to be fitted. I have all the measurements with me."

She shakes her head at me and looks down at the gown. Then her eyes widen. "Designer?"

"Yes!" I say, hoping that might win some points.

"Estavos?" she asks.

"Yes!" I yelp, impressed that she knows which house Nicholas Gravisi designs for. I didn't know until I got the dress.

She smiles at me. "Okay," she says. "Five hours."

I look at my watch—it's eleven thirty, so if it's ready by four thirty P.M. that should give me enough time to get it to Julie. I resist the urge to leap over the counter and hug the tailor. Instead I shout, "Thank you!" and hurry out the door.

I rush home and drop the keys in my dad's lap. "Violet, you're supposed to ask when you—"

"Sorry, Dad!" I shout, as I run up the stairs. "Emergency."

I immediately IM Roger.

VIOLET GREENFIELD: prom?

RC1: You sleuth!

VIOLET GREENFIELD: uh, kind of obvi when jake brings home his tux

RC1: Ah, right.

VIOLET GREENFIELD: i have a plan in the works

RC1: So do I.

VIOLET GREENFIELD: julie?

RC1: Yeah. I told her I had a mystery date, but I swore it wasn't you.

My heart sinks a little.

VIOLET GREENFIELD: so who is it?

RC1: You, Doof! But it was the only way I could figure out how to get us all together.

Yay! I can't believe I actually feel excited about the fact that I'll be going to prom with Roger. What is wrong with me?

RC1: Hello?

VIOLET GREENFIELD: sorry . . . got distracted.

VIOLET GREENFIELD: does julie have a date?

RC1: Yes. You don't know this?

VIOLET GREENFIELD: know what?

RC1: I'll tell you tonight. Anyway, what's your plan?

Violet Greenfield: i just dropped a dress off at the tailor. a Nicholas Gravisi

RC1: Are you bringing a foreign guy to the prom?

VIOLET GREENFIELD: haha. no, he's a designer. and my plan is for julie to wear it.

RC1: Genius.

VIOLET GREENFIELD: i know

VIOLET GREENFIELD: can you pick it up for me and bring it to her?

RC1: Done.

VIOLET GREENFIELD: think it'll work?

RC1: Buying friends always works, Violet.

RC1: Haha. Kidding.

RC1: I hope so.

VIOLET GREENFIELD: I do too.

twenty-seven

I'm not even tempted to put on major designer wear for the prom. I grab a red Betsy Johnson dress that I got at a sample sale with Veronica. I remember that she snorted at it because it's from two seasons ago. I still think it's cute—princess sleeves with an empire waist and a floor-length skirt. With a long gold locket necklace and metallic ballet flats, I feel just the right amount of glamour—the right amount for high school, that is. As I look in the mirror and put on mascara, I wonder if this is the outfit I would wear to prom as Violet Greenfield, high school wallflower. Probably not, but I still feel like me.

When Roger rings the doorbell, I open the door to find that he actually looks like a guy. I mean, a guy guy. Like one you might date. I step back a little because the last time we hugged I got this weird feeling—and I just want things to be back to normal tonight.

"Extra gel, Mr. Stern?" I laugh.

"I've gotta compete with that gold bling you're rocking, supermodel," he says, handing me an orchid wrist corsage. "And seriously, you look beautiful."

I can't believe I'm actually getting butterflies at a comment from Roger. But something about the utter lack of sarcasm makes me think he really means it. We stand in the entryway for a minute without saying anything.

Then Jake stomps down the steps, all decked out in black.

"Tails?" I ask.

"Tails rule!" he says. "Hey, Roger."

"Hey, Jake. So the whole team's in tails, I presume?"

"Yeah," Jake says. "Solidarity in formal wear, you know. Hey, guys, I gotta run and pick up my date."

"Who are you going with anyway?" I ask.

"Uh . . ." Jake looks at Roger.

"Actually," says Roger. "I think your date is—"

"Already here." And then I see Julie standing at the front door. She's wearing the Gravisi gown, and her hair is a cascade of dark curls falling around her shoulders. She's carrying a deep red leather clutch that matches the bow around her teeny little waist. I make a mental note to write a thank-you letter to the tailor—the dress fits perfectly.

"Whoa," says Jake. "You look amazing."

I glance away from Julie and look at my brother. Then it clicks. He's Julie's prom date. I don't have time to consider all the weirdness there, and maybe it doesn't seem so out of place. They've always liked each other.

When I turn back to Julie, she's looking at me. "Thanks for the dress, V," she says shakily.

"No one could look better in it," I say.

She leans in to hug me, and I find myself doing the New York waist-bend hug where you don't really touch the other person much. Things still feel strained, and I realize that it was stupid of me to think that a dress would make Julie actually forgive me—especially after all the crap that Shelly's been putting her through this year.

"Ah, lovely," says Roger. "Another friendship mended by fashion."

Julie backs up and hits Roger with her clutch. I guess a superficial hug is all I can expect for now.

"Dude, are we all gonna fit in the Rabbit?" says Jake, who's looking out the window at Julie's car with skepticism, totally oblivious to the emotional moment.

"It's tradition, Jake," says Roger.

"Shotgun!" shouts my brother.

"Too fast for me," says Roger, smiling. He looks at me.

"I guess we'll be sharing the backseat," I say.

"Nightmare," he says, grinning.

When we walk into the Marriott, I have to laugh. The theme is "Young Hollywood," so there are fake paparazzi outside the doors to take our photo as we enter.

"How does this compare to the real thing?" whispers Roger, as we smile for the cameras.

"Just don't give them an interview about how I'm a prude later." I laugh.

Roger smiles at me and says, "As long as you put out, there's no interview to give."

I just punch him as we walk into the ballroom. There I spy the BK talking loudly in the center of the room. When Julie, Roger, Jake, and I enter, though, they go quiet. In fact, the whole place seems to go quiet. I notice that Shelly and Brian Radcliff are holding hands, and I realize that I couldn't care less. I'm so over the crush I had on him. I look up at Roger, who's making Julie laugh by pointing out that Kelly Jones and Sophie Rushmore are wearing the same dress. I smile and squeeze his hand instinctively, and it feels so nice to hold it that I keep my hand in his for a minute as he turns to me and winks.

Then Shelly Ryan walks over to us, Jasmine and Tina trailing her as usual.

"Nice dress, Julie," Shelly says, smiling with her mouth but shooting daggers with her eyes. "Did you pick that up in New York, Violet?" She turns to me.

"Yup," I say, reluctantly dropping Roger's hand and hoping to move away from Shelly as soon as possible. I'm starting to recognize toxic people, and the BK girls are definitely radioactive. Besides, the whole school is watching us interact. I can feel it.

"So what's a big model doing home for a little old high school prom?" Shelly sneers loudly. "And, more important, why are you still hanging out with these *losers*?" She points two fingers at Roger and Julie, and I feel my heart start to beat faster with anger. While the old Violet would have slouched her shoulders and looked at her shoes, I step forward and get in Shelly's face.

"My life here is important to me, Shelly," I say. "And I needed to get away from fake people." I stare at her, then Tina, then Jasmine, lingering on each of their faces as their jaws drop. Before Shelly can strike back, Roger grabs my elbow and escorts me to the dance floor. Julie and Jake follow, snickering.

"That was awesome, Violet," says Jake.

"Classic," Julie agrees.

"I guess you learned something useful in New York after all," says Roger.

"You mean the art of the verbal bitchslap?" I laugh. "Yeah, I learned from the best."

Later that night, I sneak into the lobby to make a phone call.

"Veronica Trask's room, please," I say to the night nurse.

"V?" she says, picking up.

"V!" I say. We both laugh.

"How'd you know it was me?" I ask.

"Uh, not many phone calls," she says. "I had a feeling."

"Guess where I am?" I say.

"Where?"

"Prom!"

"No. Way." In the pause that follows, I'm almost afraid Veronica's going to make fun of me, but then she says, "I'm so jealous. I never went to my prom."

"You didn't?" I ask.

"I was shooting some stupid fashion spread," she says, sighing. "Hey wait—isn't the Voile shoot this weekend?"

"I guess," I say. "I wouldn't know. I quit."

"You quit?!" she says, sounding incredulous. "But Violet, that's the biggest campaign of the spring—it would mean so much money and exposure and—"

"I know, *Angela*," I say.

"Okay, okay," she says. "I guess I'm still in get-ahead mode."

"That's okay," I say. "I'm just not."

"What did Angela say when you told her?" asks Veronica.

"I don't know—I hung up on her right after I said I was leaving!" We both cackle nervously.

"Ballsy, Greenfield!" says Veronica. "Nice work."

"Yeah, but I'm sure she's dropped me completely by now," I say. "She's only calling once a day."

"You don't pick up?"

"Nope," I say.

"Wow, I wish I had those guts," says Veronica. "But I think I'm in the business for life. Or at least until I'm like thirty and old."

"Hey, when is your, uh, resting time over?" I ask.

"Soon!" says Veronica, perking up. "I should be in my new apartment in about two weeks."

"Your new apartment?"

"I sublet a studio in Brooklyn for the summer," she says. "I need to get away from the center of the madness, at least a little bit. Angela says people are still asking to book me, so I guess I'm not completely flatlined yet."

"Of course not!" I say, feeling so proud of Veronica for taking some control of her living situation. "Brooklyn will be just what you need."

"I hope so," says Veronica. "But you know what else I'll need?"

"What?" I ask.

"You," she says. "Are you coming back?"

"I don't think so, Veronica," I say. "But I'll visit! Aunt Rita can make us soup and maybe show us how to throw a pot one weekend. I mean, if you're up for a wild time."

Veronica laughs. "Thanks, Violet," she says. "That would be lovely."

When we hang up the phone, I go back into the ballroom to join my friends.

"Hey, can I talk to you for a minute?" asks Julie.

"Sure," I say.

We head to an empty table that's covered with shiny confetti. Julie fingers the ribbon tied to the silver balloons attached to her chair. She seems really nervous.

"Hey, Jules . . ." I start, wanting to say, again, that I feel awful about how this spring went between us and how I've been a terrible friend. How it was silly of me to think that a dress could fix all that.

"No, wait," she says. And I'm scared she's going to tell me that she hasn't forgiven me. But then she starts talking really fast. "I just wanted to say I'm sorry about not telling you I was dating Jake. It just happened like two months ago and I wanted to say something but you weren't here and we hadn't talked in a while and it just seemed like another reason to avoid you, honestly. But I really do

like him and I think we might be good for each other and of course
I already know and love your parents and . . ." She slows down for a
second. "You don't mind, do you?"

I have to stop myself from giggling because Julie looks so serious
and plaintive. "Nope," I say to her, grabbing her hand and pulling
her up to stand. "I don't mind." She smiles a huge smile and throws
her arms around me for a hug. I expect another fake hug, but Julie
pulls me in for a real one, the kind that smooshes our dresses and
could possibly have negative effects on my mascara because I'm
tearing up.

"I'm sorry," I say.

"I am too," she whispers.

The second we pull back, Julie claps her hands and starts talking
a mile a minute. "Oh, yay!" she says. "Because I think we could have
the best summer together—you and Roger, Jake and me, hanging
out constantly! Perfect, right?" I grin and realize she's got a bizarre
double-dating fantasy in her head. But we don't live in a sitcom. And
Roger and I are just old friends, I remind myself. I don't want to
make that weird just because he has guy shoulders and the way he
smells makes me slightly weak in the knees tonight. I shake my head
at Julie as we walk back to our dates—my brother is talking to the
basketball guys but I watch Julie walk over to them and I see how he
puts his arm around her, even in front of his friends. That's totally
unlike him but it makes me smile.

Later, Roger and I dance to the last song of the evening—"Wonderful Tonight" by Eric Clapton.

"Way to bring out an oldie!" says Roger. "I thought they might
end with 'Hey Ya!' or some shit and think they were being really on
top of things."

I laugh. "Roger," I say, looking in his eyes, "You're the best best-
guy-friend I could ever ask for."

I see something flash in his eyes. Disappointment? Sadness?

But his smile is quick to cover whatever it was. "Thanks, Violet," he says. "And you're the best one-of-two-best-girl-friends I could ask for."

I smile, and out of the corner of my eye I see Julie looking at us from across the dance floor. I sigh and lean onto Roger's shoulder as we slowly sway back and forth. It's good to be home.

epilogue

I don't get to walk at graduation because technically I got my diploma in December, but I watch my friends from the stadium stands and I couldn't feel happier. I am looking forward to a whole summer at home. Working at the movie theater, hanging out with Roger and Julie—who knew such regular things would seem like paradise to me after the year I've had?

I'm heading outside to meet Roger and drive to an after-graduation party when my phone rings—"You're So Vain." I'm in such a happy moment that I decide to pick up.

"Hello?"

"Vexing Violet!" trills Angela. "Where are you? At Aunt Rita's? I've got someone in town who wants to meet you."

"Angela," I say. "I'm at home, remember? In North Carolina." She's so damaged—she doesn't even acknowledge that I haven't picked up a phone call from her in weeks. I know she's talked to my mom, who's told her a few times that since the date on my original

Tryst contract has expired, I'm not coming back to New York. At least not for a while.

"Don't bore me with the details, darling!" she shoots back. "Listen, I'll tell Dona that you can't meet him this week, but he'll want to see you before he sets up his show's lineup."

"Dona?" I stammer. "Show's lineup?"

"Dona Pink, darling," she says. "The up-and-coming Brazilian bikini designer. He wants you for his São Paulo show this summer. He says only you will do, and he wants you to close the show. If you do well, we'll book fall shows overseas—maybe even Paris."

"But Angela," I say, "I can't. I'm spending the summer at home and—" As I list all the reasons why I can't possibly come back, part of me is thrilled at the idea that an international designer requested me personally. To go to Brazil! "And I'm going to college in the fall," I finish, not even quite convincing myself. "What about college?" I wonder aloud.

"One word, Valued Violet," says Angela. "Defer."

And now a special excerpt of the
next book in the Violet series . . .

violet by design

Coming from Berkley JAM
March 2008!!!

By the time I go through baggage claim and customs in São Paulo, I'm so tired that I can barely read my own name, which is on a sign being held by a short, gray-haired man with a curled-up mustache. We pantomime a bit to determine that, yes, I am Violet Greenfield. Lamely, I had been thinking my high school Spanish might be useful in Brazil, but—duh—they speak Portuguese here.

As we drive through the city, I can't help but think it looks a lot like New York—giant buildings everywhere, crowds and busy streets, bicycles weaving in and out of traffic. When we pull up to the Mirna Hotel, I feel like a little girl pretending she's old enough to be jet-setting and staying in fancy places. The concierge speaks English perfectly, and as the bellhop rides up to my room with me, I get a tingle of excitement. I am in *another country*. I look down at my brown-suede ballet flats and flash back to them walking down my driveway just this morning. Now they're standing in an old-fashioned, gold-gilt-covered elevator in *Brazil*.

We get off the elevator on the seventh floor, and I realize the whole hotel opens in the middle around a giant, curving staircase like in *Gone With the Wind*—which, okay, is my secret favorite movie. (My public favorite movie is *The Royal Tenenbaums*, which, while a great film with infinitely more cool cred, is no *Gone With the Wind*.) The man helping me with my suitcase—who is wearing a red military jacket that doesn't look that far off from what I wore on a runway last winter—opens the door to room 704 and places my suitcases on a folding wooden luggage stand that looks like it's from my grandmother's house—in a good way. Then he bows and holds out his hand. I shake it, smiling at him and saying, "Obrigada," which is the one word the cab driver managed to drill into my head—it means "thank you." Then he shuffles out the door and I turn around and take a deep breath.

My room is gorgeous. Tiny, but "just lovely," as I can hear my mom saying. Burnt-orange organza curtains hang across a huge window that looks out onto the sparkling São Paulo skyline. The shower is all glass, and there are silver beads on the outside of the panel that faces the bed, which I suppose is for giving the illusion of privacy. The bathroom floors are marble, and I find out after playing with an assortment of buttons on the wall that they are also— dramatic pause—*heated*! My feet are always cold, so I especially appreciate the warmth. I have a little refrigerator with candy and water and wine in it—not to mention a giant fruit bowl on the desk in the corner, where apples and oranges and grapes and bananas are arranged around a large bottle of champagne.

But the really exciting stuff is on my bed. Not my bed itself, which is cute and covered with a grass-patterned green-and-gray down comforter, but what's *on* my bed. Presents! There must be fifty bags with tissue paper sticking out of the tops—blue and pink and yellow and green, all with tags that say "Violet Greenfield" or "Bela Violeta" or simply "VG," which sort of looks cool in calligraphy. Inside are invitations to attend fashion shows, personal letters from designers, and lots—I mean lots—of free stuff. A pair of dark-wash high-waist jeans from Ellys, an amazing long-sleeved eyelet lace dress from Ingrid Cupola, and four new bikinis from Dona Pink, to name a few. As I tear through package after package, I think I feel a swag headache coming on. This must be how movie stars feel when they get their Oscar gift bags. I lie back on the tissue paper with a sigh.

Brring, brring. The phone does a double-time ring and totally scares me. I haven't called my parents yet to give them my number—who else could it be? I reach over to grab it. "Hello?"

"Valiant Violet." It's my agent.

"Hi, Angela," I say, almost happy to hear her voice. I was worried I was going to have to stumble through "You've got the wrong number" in Portuguese.

"Darling, what's that rustling?" she asks.

"Uh, gift bags," I say sheepishly, wondering if it's weird to open all of them at once like it's Christmas morning. I bet most international runway models are so used to the presents that they just put them aside and barely glance at the goodies inside. I'm so not at that too-cool point, and I kind of doubt I ever will be.

"Well get yourself out of that mess," Angela orders. "We've got an appointment at the hotel spa in five minutes. I'll see you downstairs."

Click. Ooh, the spa sounds nice. I pull on my yoga pants and a T-shirt and head downstairs.

"Greetings, Sporty Spice," says Angela, as she air kisses both my cheeks. She doesn't say it in a nice way. Her blond hair is perfectly highlighted and blown out, as always, and her gleaming red lipstick matches well-manicured hands. "You know, even at the spa we do like to wear real clothes."

I feel my shoulders start to shrink in a little. I forgot how much Angela's criticisms sting sometimes.

"Oh, toughen up, Vulnerable Violet," she says. "You'll need thick skin for this appointment."

"What is it for?" I ask, suddenly terrified.

"What else?" says Angela, smiling wickedly. "A Brazilian!"

After a few tears and some pitiful whining, I agreed that it did make sense for me to go through with the ritual of torture known as the Brazilian bikini wax, and that Brazil was probably the best place to do it. I am modeling swimsuits, after all. Angela said she knew she'd have to drag me kicking and screaming to the table, so she hadn't dared ask me to get one on my own at home. "Besides," she said, "who knows what those country-bumpkin spa women would have done to you."

Back in my hotel room, I'm lotioning and icing my throbbing, red bikini line. Oh yes, it hurt. When I walked back through the lobby with Angela, I looked like a cowboy in a John Wayne movie who'd been riding his horse for ten days straight. Just as the pain is starting to subside, my phone rings.

"Get dressed," Angela barks. "I'll meet you in the lobby in five."

"Dressed?" I stammer.

"For dinner, of course," snaps Angela. "We'll be dining with a few designers and some other Tryst girls tonight."

I can feel my underarms start to sweat as my heart beats faster.

"Oh, and Violet?" purrs Angela. "When you're throwing on a dress, think Lower East Side—not Lower Atlantic Coast." And then she's gone.

And I'm panicked.

I slip on a simple black shift dress with long sleeves, but I leave my coat in the room. Contrary to my mom's assessment that the July winter in Brazil would be cold, it only dips into the sixties at night—and it's like seventy during the day, I hear. Guess I should have Googled that one myself. Dinner is in the garden of a restaurant just down the block from the hotel, which is good because I'm wearing red patent leather heels that are "too cute for words" according to Julie, but "too painful for words" according to me. Still, I trust my best friend's assessment and I want to look good tonight. I manage to walk normally because the trauma of my wax experience has faded somewhat, and I even put on a long gold chain necklace that Veronica once told me was "edgy but feminine," so I feel like I'm pulling off the look Angela wanted. When she sees me, however, she just chirps, "Well, good enough!" before she hurries me out the door of the hotel. So much for my confidence.

The restaurant is called Spot and we're seated at a long table in front of the blue-green-yellow Brazilian flag, which is as ubiquitous here as the American flag is in rural parts of North Carolina. The room is enclosed in glass, and the crowd of beautiful people is buzzing with energy. I like it because it reminds me that I'm in a completely new world where I should take everything in.

But what I'm taking in now are all the girls at the table, some of whom are chattering in Portuguese and others who are sitting sullenly, staring at the bread basket with longing eyes. I guess that's what I'm doing too, but only because I don't want to be the only one who eats the bread.

I glance around the table and try to remember a few of the flurry of names Angela rattled off when we sat down. There's Amelia and Lucy, models from New York whom I've seen before but who completely intimidate me with their vacant eyes, and then two Brazilian models with exotic names—Vidonia and Yelena maybe? I can't remember who is who. At the far end of the table is Dona Pink himself, the flamboyant bikini designer who requested me for his show and single-handedly relaunched my modeling career with the promise of this trip to Brazil. He has unkempt black hair that frames his ultratan face a bit wildly, and he's wearing a button-down shirt that is open almost to the navel. He sort of seems like a gay Brazilian Elvis, which is pretty entertaining. He sees me looking at him and raises his glass, shouting, "Violeta!" at which all the other girls reluctantly pick up their drinks and join the toast to me. I blush a little and hold up my Caipirinha, which is a traditional Brazilian drink that tastes limey and has a lot of sugar in it. Translation: I love it. And I've already had two to calm my nerves.

I'm sitting next to Angela at the edge of the table when someone takes the head seat on my left. I look over and see the deepest brown eyes I've witnessed since those of my neighbor's golden retriever. I know it sounds odd to compare dog eyes to person eyes, but believe me, it's a compliment. He also has this adorable, shiny, floppy brown hair that falls just above his shoulders. The guy, not the dog. And he's got big, soft pink lips. "Hello, Violet," he says quietly, as he sits down, as though he wants only me to hear his greeting. I feel my eyelashes flutter involuntarily, and I nervously place my hand on my drink to steady its shaking. Suddenly I am acutely aware of how bare I feel, uh, down there. *Am I drunk?* I wonder. Although I did learn to throw a few back in New York last year, I didn't really drink all summer in North Carolina. My tolerance must be way low.

"Hello," I respond, wishing I knew his name too, but so flattered he knows who I am. After going through life as a high school wallflower, it's still a shock when people get my name right—even now. Especially people who are, oh, drop-dead gorgeous.

Then Beautiful Boy begins to speak: "My name is . . ."

Go back to school in style
with Berkley Jam

Girls That Growl (Available October 2007)
by Mari Mancusi
Third in this hip, sassy vampire series.

Demon Envy (Available October 2007)
by Erin Lynn
Being a teenager can be hell—especially if you're friends
with someone who was born there.

Queen Geeks in Love (Available November 2007)
by Laura Preble
"Give the nerd in you a chance to get up and shout" (*Girls'
Life* magazine) with the second book in this fresh series.

The Band: Finding Love (Available November 2007)
by Debra Garfinkle
Catch up with the hit band Amber Road as they navigate
their newfound fame—and their fragile emotions.

Manderley Prep: A BFF Novel (Available December 2007)
by Carol Culver
Welcome to exclusive academy of Manderley Prep, where
the only thing harder than the classes is fitting in.

Go to penguin.com to order!